Doris Fein:
Deadly Aphrodite

Doris Fein: Deadly Aphrodite

T. Ernesto Bethancourt

Holiday House / New York

Library of Congress Cataloging in Publication Data

Bethancourt, T. Ernesto
  Doris Fein, deadly Aphrodite.

SUMMARY: Doris checks into a very exclusive health
spa and discovers that someone is systematically doing
away with the world's wealthiest women. With the help
of Larry Small she begins to unravel a seven-year-old
murder mystery.
  [1. Mystery and detective stories] I. Title.
PZ7.B46627Don   [Fic]   81–85093
ISBN 0–8234–0445–5   AACR2

For Mel Rosenberg,
one of Doris Fein's first gentleman admirers,
and dear friend of Doris's daddy

Contents

Doris Fein:
Deadly Aphrodite

1/ The Incredible Growing Fein

"Doris Fein, you are gross!" I said to my reflection in the three-paneled mirror. "You look like a pink Mount Everest." I walked over to the towel cabinet and took out an oversized white bath sheet that bore the monogram *G* near its satin hem. Wrapping it around me, I returned to the mirror.

"Now you look like Everest after a snowfall," said my reflection. "Face it, Ms. Fein," she went on, "you have eaten yourself to the very brink of half sizes again."

"Don't be smart," I replied. "No one loves a wiseass."

"And no one loves a blimp, either," retorted my reflection.

I turned my back on the offensive young person in the mirror and busied myself with drying off. I avoided the sight of myself, which was hard to do. Two entire walls of the master bathroom in Harry Grubb's mansion are mirrored. The floors are travertine marble, somehow always mysteriously heated. The sunken marble tub could accommodate a small power launch in its depths. I don't know what a stranger to that tub would fear more: falling asleep and drowning or a submarine attack.

Funny, I keep thinking of the place as Harry Grubb's mansion. Actually, it's mine. All twenty-six rooms, not counting the guest house and servants' apartments above the six-car garage. Now, before you begin to think that I am to the manor born, think again.

I was born eighteen years ago, to Dr. Michael and Linda Fein, in Santa Amelia, California. That's in Southern California, in Orange County. My dad is a hardworking ophthalmologist, and for years, my mom was his nurse and receptionist. In fact, I was my dad's receptionist for my last eighteen months in Santa Amelia High School so I could earn the money to get my TR-7 sports car. I dubbed it the Flying Gumdrop because it's gumdrop green and looks like it's going a hundred miles an hour, even when it's standing still.

All right, you say. She's a nice middle-class Jewish girl from Southern California. What's she doing in someone's mansion, emerging from a sybaritic bath? I wonder at it myself. No, I am not a "kept" woman. I am my own person, and of voting age. Nobody owns Doris Fein but Ms. Fein, thank you. But I am rich now. Richer than I ever could have dreamed.

I inherited the whole setup from a comparative stranger, a man named Harry Grubb. Harry was one of the richest and most eccentric men in Southern California. He owned this incredible house, which is filled with *objets d'art*. It has sections and rooms to it that I'm still exploring. Even now, months after Harry's death.

When I had finished drying off, I took a cerise terry cloth robe from a wall hook, slipped into matching terry scuffs, and walked through the spacious master bedroom. I don't use the master bedroom. It's so completely an expression of Harry Grubb that I couldn't bear to. My bedroom is down the hall. It has a separate bathroom, but it's not the Roman wallow of delights that Harry had installed for his own use. Harry was close to six feet, four inches tall, and everything in his bathroom and bedroom is oversized. I'd feel like one of the seven dwarfs in the huge, canopied four-poster that dominates his bedroom. My bedroom is the one room in the house that I decorated. No decorator came in to do it either, though my lawyer says I could have afforded one. In fact, I can afford just about anything I want. But all I did was have the furniture from my bedroom at home moved to Harry's mansion in Santa Amelia Estates.

It's a bit incongruous to walk into my room after seeing all the art work and other stuff that fills the mansion. My room is right out of a nice middle-class Southern California home, right down to the picture of Danny Breckinridge, or Dr. Doom, the rock singer, on the wall. It's an autographed picture. I once helped Danny out of a nasty mess that included blackmail and the murder of his bass player.

That's how I met Harry Grubb to begin with. I was star reporter on *The Blade,* the school newspaper at Santa Amelia High. Harry was the crime reporter on *The Register,* the town's daily newspaper, when the attempt on Danny Breckinridge's life was made. I and Larry Small, who wrote a column on rock music for the school paper, were covering the Dr. Doom concert when it all happened. Harry was covering the concert because of some threatening letters Danny had received. Among us, we solved the mystery.

Larry later wrote a novel about the Dr. Doom case, which was such a success that he got what he'd always wanted: a job on the staff of *Rolling Stone* magazine in San Francisco.

The Dr. Doom case was the beginning of a loving adversary relationship between Harry and me. In the months that followed, we both became involved in a couple of other cases. A friendship, based on mutual respect, grew out of them. Remarkable, considering that Harry was close to eighty years old, and Old Guard. With capital letters.

I changed my robe for an outsized sweat shirt with a picture of Felix Mendelssohn on it and a new pair of jeans. My old ones didn't fit anymore. I picked up the phone and buzzed the kitchen on the intercom.

"Yes, Ms. Fein?" came Bruno's voice over the intercom.

"I'll be down for breakfast in five minutes."

"Very good, Ms. Fein. Eggs Benedict this morning."

"Fine with me, Bruno," I said and replaced the phone, feeling a twinge of guilt about the rich meal awaiting me.

I made a few passes at my hair with a brush and decided to wrap it in a towel. My hair, that is. It was still damp from the steamy tub anyhow. Besides, who was going to see me but Bruno? There were a half-dozen day workers around the grounds, but Bruno is the majordomo, strongarm, and chef. He doesn't like too many people inside the house. He says it's a matter of security. Harry wasn't one to hide valuable art objects in vaults. He wanted his things out in plain view so he could see them and touch them whenever he liked. I saw no reason to change all that.

I took the service stairs down to the kitchen. It's easier, and most of the time I eat in the kitchen. I think Bruno disapproves of both practices. But I'll be darned if I'll eat alone in the dining room. It's huge. As it is, half the time I feel like Orson Welles in *Citizen Kane,* rattling around, surrounded by opulence, yet *verry* alone.

Bruno had the table set with linen and a floral centerpiece, silver from the ordinary service, and our day-to-day Doulton china. In a Baccarat crystal glass was my orange juice. My morning mail was on a silver dish alongside my coffee cup. You see, I won the battle to eat in the kitchen. But Bruno won the war. Amid the brass, copper, and stainless steel of the kitchen, he sets up the meals as though I were eating in the formal dining room.

I sipped my orange juice. It was fresh-squeezed. I gave in to Bruno on that, too. Even I could see how gauche it would be to have a Baccarat crystal glassful of Tang. I didn't bother greeting Bruno as he served my meal. I wouldn't have gotten any conversation in return. I've rarely heard Bruno speak two consecutive sentences. But he makes himself understood. He's a convicted murderer, you know.

I just say that for effect. Bruno is a man who was *wrongly* convicted of murder, years ago, in Chicago. Harry Grubb was on the staff of the *Chicago Tribune* at the time. He covered the murders and Bruno's trial. He never believed the charges. He kept scratching and eventually won Bruno a full pardon. He also won a Pulitzer Prize nomination for the story. Had he won, it would have been his second Pulitzer.

Bruno had already served twenty-five years in a hospital for the criminally insane before Harry was able to clear him. His devotion to Harry was understandable. So much so that when Harry asked him, in his will, to stay on and take care of things, he did so. Harry left Bruno well off, but I guess in Bruno's mind, he's still carrying out Harry's wishes. With a vengeance. He maintains the house exactly as Harry used to like it. That sort of devotion. Harry had only to express some wish, and Bruno would go at it with a ferocious singularity of purpose.

I'll give you an example. When Harry expressed a desire for *haute cuisine,* the finest in French cooking, Bruno promptly studied and became a master chef. I'm serious. No, he didn't go away to a cooking school. Harry paid a master French chef to live in for a year and teach Bruno. In a way, Bruno was responsible for the fact that I was rapidly beginning to resemble Shamu, the whale at Sea World. The other culprit in the saga of the Incredible Growing Fein was Petunia.

Petunia is my alter ego. Doris Fein is a nice, sensible person who is either a teensy bit overweight or at times fifteen pounds above the mark. Doris Fein watches the intake and eats sensibly. *Petunia* Fein, on the other hand, has food in *each* hand. Her idea of a light snack is dinner.

But for the past few months, Petunia had gotten completely out of hand. I won't kid you about the shape I was in. I was verging on shapeless. I was eating out of loneliness and the old insecurities that had so plagued my early years. The result then was the same. I ended up with a shape like the Blob, and with a mouthful of braces. And zits. And tears and self-pity. You name it; I had it all. Except dates.

Even when I'm in fighting trim, I'm hardly the typical Southern California sex symbol. All the girls out here try to look like Barbie dolls. And all the boys look like Barbie's boyfriend, Ken. But with surfboards. Some of the girls look so plastic that if they didn't have navels showing above their bikini bottoms, you'd think they were manufactured.

I toyed with my eggs Benedict and thought back to the events three months ago that had brought me to this particular breakfast table. I had to admit they strained the imagination. Harry's death had been a shock. I'd always thought of him as indestructible. He'd lived for so many years, and survived so many major historical events. Sort of like my history teacher at Santa Amelia High, Mrs. Hornbeck. When she taught history, you tended to believe her. She looked as though she'd seen it all firsthand.

Harry had been a crime reporter and a bachelor for most of his adult life. It wasn't until he was sixty that he got married, to one of the richest widows in Chicago.

Ironically, the marriage lasted only a little over a year, because she died. Harry found himself immensely wealthy, but with no direction. He'd left his job on the *Chicago Tribune* and was too old to go out looking for a fresh start.

He came to Santa Amelia about twelve years ago. He was going to write his memoirs. But he found out that what he did best was crime reporting. In his own sulfurous words, the memoirs turned out to be "Crap! Pure, artsy, pretentious crap. . . ." For a time, he enjoyed his new-found wealth. He bought and restored this huge mansion I now live in. He helped finance the Santa Amelia Municipal Arena. He acquired controlling interest in the Saints, our basketball team. In the end, he was terribly bored. All he really knew how to do, or wanted to do, was be a crime reporter.

So he bought *The Register,* which I own now, just so he could hire himself to be the ace crime reporter. He brought in Dave Rose to be editor, all the way from Toledo, Ohio. In consequence of Harry's efforts, *The Register* is one of the most modern and successful papers in our county.

Even though Harry complained about it, he did a great deal to improve the quality of life in Santa Amelia. Good works, various charities and arts associations; all anonymous. But when he left me his money after he died while covering a fire in downtown Santa Amelia, I can't say that he improved the quality of *my* life.

For one thing, my new-found wealth alienated me from Carl Suzuki. Carl is an assistant district attorney in New York these days. But when we met there a year ago, he was a detective on the New York police force. We got involved in a terrorist plot that nearly resulted in my death. In the process, we became *verry* close. In fact, Carl even proposed marriage. But once the money came into my life, his feelings changed.

Not about me, but my money. Carl is Japanese-American and an extremely proud and honor-bound man. He told me that if he were to marry a fortune (an interesting way of putting it, rather than saying "a *person* with a fortune"), he'd never know whether his personal successes were valid or a result of my wealth and influence. When he walked out of my life, it hurt deeply.

Once the news of my inheritance hit the newspapers, my life at U.C.I. (The University of California at Irvine) changed, too. All of a sudden little campus "in groups" began to approach me. Before that, outside of a few friends from Santa Amelia High, I could have been the Unknown Soldier, slogging through the halls. But that wasn't all.

I began to get offers for dinner and dancing from all the surfboard-and-Porsche guys. Well, maybe some of them were interested in me personally. I'd like to think so. In fact, I agonized a great deal about it. Told myself that my childhood insecurities were blocking the way to my meeting interesting and handsome men. But after a few dinners with a sampling of them, I stopped going out.

Funny, I always wondered what it would be like to go places and be seen with those Greek gods I'd watched for my entire miserable early teens. I may have picked the wrong ones to go with, but generally, an evening with those beautiful, empty-headed guys was like a day of watching a tree grow. That stimulating.

I began to stay closer to my new, huge house. I can't bring myself to call it home. It was Harry's home, and still is, to me. Only my room, with my own things in it, seems like home. The fact that whenever I so much as move something, Bruno puts it back where Harry originally had it doesn't help, either. I don't go into Harry's office-cum-library anymore. Bruno keeps it like a shrine. I'm afraid of disturbing something.

Yes, yes, I know. Poor little rich girl. Up to her well-upholstered rear in luxury, and yet complaining. Well, what of it? Whoever it was who said that money brings happiness may have been right. I know that if I had *earned* all my new belongings, I would have enjoyed them to the hilt. I was beginning to understand why Harry acted the way he did about his money. *He* had inherited it, after a lifetime of slogging away as a reporter. Another Unknown Soldier. Except that an unknown doesn't win a Pulitzer Prize. Harry had a solid career of genuine accomplishments to buffer the impact of his inheritance.

I finished breakfast and the morning edition of *The Register.* Picking up my mail, I gave a start. I didn't have to look at the return address to know who'd sent one of the letters. I recognized the handwriting immediately. It was from Larry Small in San Francisco. I felt a sudden rush of warmth and affection. Larry had cared for me when I was plain old lumpy Doris Fein, poor but proud. I opened the envelope with the silver letter opener Bruno always puts on the mail tray.

Dear Dee, it began. (I'm afraid that's what Larry calls me, since my dad's pet name for me is Dee-Dee. Because Larry and I grew up together, he knows me better than anyone outside my family.)

San Francisco wasn't exactly the end of the rainbow, the letter continued, *but I have made my mark up here. The music scene is as wild as the parties. They keep me busy at* Rolling Stone, *but not so busy that I don't think of home and you.*

I swallowed hard at that line. All the memories came rushing back. The times Larry and I had together. Some of them scary and some quite . . . well, that's another story, isn't it?

The letter went on to say: *I won't be going back to Santa Amelia for Thanksgiving this year. Too much popping on the set here. But I am definitely going home for the Christmas holidays. If you ain't too rich to talk to us commoners nowadays, maybe we can get together for a concert or a flick, okay? I'll be getting into town December 20th. That's a Monday, and will stay until after New Year's. Maybe longer.*

The day suddenly seemed brighter. Larry was coming home in six weeks . . . no, seven and a half.

"Bruno?"

"Yes, Ms. Fein?" he said, and I jumped. He was standing directly behind me. He's so darned silent, you forget he's there sometimes. I spun around.

"Were you reading my mail over my shoulder?" I asked.

"No, Ms. Fein," he replied in his chatterbox fashion. Then, to my embarrassment, he began to clear away the remains of my breakfast. He'd been hovering nearby, waiting to clear off the table.

"I've had some good news, Bruno," I said quickly, hiding my flushed face. I'm afraid I *do* blush easily. "It's about time we did some entertaining here," I said firmly. "We are going to have company for dinner."

"Mr. Grubb didn't entertain often," Bruno said flatly, as though I was talking about desecrating the premises.

I mentally set my teeth. Either I owned this place or I didn't. I'd be darned if I was going to spend the rest of my time here being pushed around by Harry Grubb's ghost, as personified by Bruno. The way Joan Fontaine in *Rebecca* was bullied by her creepy housekeeper.

"Mr. Grubb is no longer with us, Bruno," I said.

"Yes, Ms. Fein."

"Yes, he is?" I came back, "or yes, he isn't?"

"Both, Ms. Fein," he answered, clearing off the last of the dishes. And darnit! I had to admit he was right, in a way. But I was committed.

"I'll be inviting my parents, my Uncle Saul and Aunt Ceil," I said, counting off guests on my fingers. "I'll also want to invite Dave Rose, and that new crime reporter . . . what's his name?"

"Kobrin, Ms. Fein. Jerry Kobrin."

"Yes, him. Dave hired him two months ago, and I still haven't met him." I paused and thought. "Dave says this Kobrin fellow likes a good meal. I think a beef Wellington might be the thing, Bruno."

"Yes, Ms. Fein."

I thought of Bruno's beef Wellington, and just as Petunia gave a grunt of anticipation, I said, "And a Caesar salad for me, Bruno."

I made up my mind then. I'd wallowed in self-pity long enough. I was going to shed the tonnage and be back in shape by December. Larry Small was coming home!

2/ Enter Jerry Kobrin

"Are you men going to shoot pool all night, or are we going to have dinner some time soon?" asked my Aunt Ceil.

"One more shot . . ." said my father, sinking the eight ball in a corner pocket. The ball rolled in without touching the sides of the pocket and clicked into the basket of woven leather below. "Gotcha again, Saul!" he crowed. "You now owe me two dinners."

"Swell," boomed my Uncle Saul. "We can start with this one."

"It doesn't count, Saul," my father replied. "This is Doris's treat."

"It's a treat if you get to eat it," Ceil interjected.

We were in the billiard room of the big house. Dave Rose and the new crime reporter, Jerry Kobrin, had called to say they'd be late. A late-breaking story Jerry had to cover, and the usual unwillingness to leave the paper's offices on Dave's part had accounted for their

16

tardiness. I had polled the guests for dinner: my folks, Uncle Saul, and Aunt Ceil. We'd decided to wait until the rest of the party arrived. It hadn't been much of a decision. Once Dad had seen Harry's antique pool table, the issue was settled. My dad is a pool nut. We've had a small table in our family room ever since I can remember.

Dad likes the game so much that he taught me how to play when I was old enough to hold a cue stick. As a result, I play very well, but not nearly as well as Dad. He claims that when he was an intern, he courted Mom with the money he made shooting pool. Interns back then, as now, hardly make any money. I can believe his claim. The world lost a great pool hustler when Michael Fein chose to take up medicine.

Dad's favorite quarry is Uncle Saul. He's my dad's brother, but to look at them together, you'd think they might be distantly related. Dad is a shade under six feet tall, with an athletic build and a full head of hair, salt-and-pepper variety. Uncle Saul is the same height, but easily fifty pounds heavier and, except for a fringe of hair, is bald. He is one of the most relentlessly good-natured men I have ever known. Dad is fond of saying that Uncle Saul could live in a nest of rattlesnakes and never get bitten.

I agree. I can see him now, telling a six-foot rattler to "Open wide, please," while he drilled a fang with a cavity. Uncle Saul is a dentist, and responsible for my best feature, my teeth. He gets along with anyone. It's just as well. My Aunt Ceil is hard to take sometimes. She was a professional ice skater with Ice Follies years ago.

I suppose the star treatment she gets from Uncle Saul is what makes her think she's still a headliner, surrounded by adoring fans. She is an attractive woman in her early forties who is losing the war on calories. Going from professional athletics to a life of little or no exercise can do that to you.

I sighed. Thinking of Aunt Ceil's slight weight problem made me more acutely aware of the weight I had gained.

"Something wrong, honey?" my mom asked, hearing my sigh.

"No, not at all," I said.

"She's probably as hungry as I am," Aunt Ceil said with her usual tact. She gave me a hard look. "But you look well fed enough, my dear," she added mercilessly. I was about to make a comment on Jewish-American princesses when the gate buzzer rang.

The big, old house sits on two and a half fenced acres. There is a wall that runs its circumference, with a big, wrought-iron gate leading to the driveway. To gain access, you have to ring one of those interviewer thingies down at the entry. I heard Bruno answer, and heard the little beep that the interviewer makes when you push the GATE OPEN button. In a moment, Bruno came into the billiard room.

"Guests," he announced. My aunt nearly jumped out of her skin. She had been facing away from the door when Bruno entered. I've gotten used to the silent way Bruno has of walking. But it is eerie, the way he cat-foots it around the house.

"We'll meet them at the door, Bruno," I said. "Are the Rover Boys loose?"

"Always, after dark," Bruno replied.

"Call them in, then, Bruno," I said.

"Yes, Ms. Fein," Bruno quipped, and went off to call in the two Alsatian shepherd dogs that roam the place, patrolling for interlopers. Harry named them the Rover Boys and called each of them Rover. He said that because they were identical, there was no point in giving them separate names. I feel that taking a beautiful animal like a shepherd and turning it into a ferocious thing like a guard dog is a perversion.

But once I owned the Rover Boys, and spent weeks with their original trainer learning the ins and outs of guard-dog education, I came to love both of them. The dogs, that is. The trainer was a middle-aged tweedy lady from Torrance who owns a school and kennel.

We all trooped out of the billiard room and into the foyer, just as Bruno opened the front door.

I don't know what I expected the new crime reporter to look like. Certainly, Harry Grubb hadn't been what you'd expect. If you expected him to look like Jack Lemmon in *Front Page,* that is. But the new reporter was an even less likely candidate, physically. When he stood alongside Dave Rose, who is short and of average build, Dave looked almost insignificant.

Jerry Kobrin is six feet tall and bearded, and weighs easily two hundred pounds. He is balding and, I'd guess, in his fifties. He was wearing a venerable tweed jacket, baggy gray slacks, a white shirt open at the collar, and what looked like Earth-shoe loafers on his feet. To top it all off, he was smoking a calabash pipe, like Sherlock Holmes. He could have been Mycroft Holmes, the older, fatter brother of Sherlock. Dave made the introductions; he knows my family. Jerry Kobrin gave me a warm, firm, and dry handshake and said, "Do you think it's safe all of us being here?"

"What do you mean?" I asked.

Jerry looked about him and said with an impish smile, "I think we're the only Jews you can find in Santa Amelia Estates." He looked about again at the opulence of the house. "But if this is ghettoizing," he added, "I think I can bear up."

I had to laugh, despite the ethnic implication. It's true. Santa Amelia Estates, the richest part of Santa Amelia, was a WASP holdout area for years. Oh, nothing overt. No signs saying KEEP OUT. But all of us knew who lived in the Estates and who didn't.

"You certainly know the area for one so recently arrived," I said, still smiling.

"It's sheer survival, Ms. Fein," Kobrin replied. "One can't be a crime reporter in a town where you can't find police headquarters. Dave has been giving me a crash course in local geography and history."

"And he's a very quick study," Dave said.

"And I am very hungry," Aunt Ceil said. As if on cue, Bruno materialized from behind the dining room doors, opening them wide. "Dinner," he said, somewhat superfluously. We went in directly.

"Magnificent!" Jerry Kobrin sighed, putting down his dessert spoon. "I'll pay for this, I know." He patted his ample midsection.

"I won't tell if you don't," said Uncle Saul with a laugh. He waved an arm thick as a tree trunk. "If you eat with fat people, you can enjoy without a guilty conscience."

"Speak for yourself, Saul," Aunt Ceil said tartly. "My old costumes still fit me."

"If you don't move or sit down, that is," I said. I'm sorry, I am not a nasty person. But, darnit, sometimes Ceil Fein gets to me.

"Now, now," Dad said, "we don't need a cat fight."

"You mean a fat fight, don't you?" roared Uncle Saul. He dissolved into gales of laughter. Uncle Saul has a deep, resonant laugh, and when he lets it go, you have to join in. The tension of the moment eased immediately. Then I heard from Mom, of all people.

"Ceil *is* a bit overweight, Doris," she said, "but if I were you, I'd not have brought up the subject." She gazed at me pointedly.

I looked up at the ceiling and said to the ornate crystal chandelier, "I know, Mom, I am carrying too much weight. That's why I only had a salad while all of you were wolfing down the beef Wellington. This dinner party is like Nebuchadnezzar's feast."

"Eat, drink and be merry, for tomorrow we diet?" Jerry Kobrin asked.

"You got it, ace reporter," I replied. "Tomorrow the battle begins."

"My deepest sympathies," Kobrin said, raising a glass of Château Lafitte Rothschild '67. "If your man Bruno cooks like this all the time, you have your work cut out for you. Myself, I'd just relax and roll with the flow, as they say here in California."

"That's the problem," I said. "If I keep up like this, they'll have to roll me out the doors at U.C.I." Bruno began clearing off the table.

"Bruno," Jerry asked, "can you make zabaglione?"

"Yes, sir," Bruno answered. "Do you want it hot or cold?"

Zabaglione is a superrich Italian dessert. Sort of a meringue flavored with Marsala wine. It's so caloric, I can gain weight being in the same room with a dish of it.

"No, no!" Jerry protested. "I don't want any. I just wanted to know if you made it." He smiled ruefully. "I haven't had any since I left the *New York Post.* I think of it, wistfully, from time to time."

"I thought Doris said you're from Reading, Pennsylvania," my dad said. "That's a good distance from New York."

Jerry smiled. "Reading is a good distance from anyplace but Harrisburg or Scranton. I did seven years on the *Post* before they changed ownership. Ah, but the restaurants in New York. There's a town for an eater!"

"Considering the swell meal we've had," Uncle Saul said, "and that Doris is going on her diet tomorrow, I think any more food talk is in bad taste!" He laughed again.

"Will you be seeing Dr. Ron first, dear?" my mother

asked. "You should have a complete checkup before starting any diet, you know."

"Yes, Mom," I said. "I've made an appointment for tomorrow morning."

"Well, don't eat any of his French fries," Uncle Saul said and roared with laughter. Jerry Kobrin looked puzzled while everyone laughed except for him and me.

"You're new in town, Jerry," I explained. "My dad has an associate at his medical group. His name is Dr. McDonald."

"*Ronald* McDonald?" Kobrin asked. "Like on the commercials?"

"I'm afraid so," my dad said. "Poor man. He's one of the better internists in the county, too. But how can you take a man seriously when he's got a name like that?" Despite himself, Dad laughed. Jerry Kobrin did, too. So hard that he reached under his eyeglasses with a corner of his napkin and dabbed at his eyes.

"With a name like that," he said between giggles, "he should be in pediatrics. I can see him treating kids in a clown suit!"

"He's a very nice man," I said, "in his fifties. He had that name long before McDonald's was in business." Then I got an attack of the sillies myself. Aunt Ceil, as ever, broke the spell.

"I'm glad to hear you're being sensible, Doris," she said nastily. "When you have all that weight to lose, you *should* see a doctor first. I, for example, just have to use a little restraint. I'm back to normal in a week or so."

"I'll be a sylph by Christmastime," I said determinedly. "By New Year's, I may buy a new wardrobe."

"That's in just a few months," Ceil said. "Are you going to check in at Aphrodite's?" She gazed about the room. "Well, I guess you can afford it. With all the money you have now."

"Fill me in," Dave said. "What's this Aphrodite's?"

"You're not on top of the weight-loss scene, Dave," I said. "Aunt Ceil is talking about the place down the road from here. You know, at the old Burroughs Estate?"

"Of course," Dave said, putting a palm to his brow. "We wrote them up when they opened five years ago. But they don't advertise in the paper, and they keep a very low profile."

"They don't have to advertise," Aunt Ceil said, "since people from all over the world go there to lose weight. Their biggest appeal is that nobody knows who their clients are. The richest women in the world check in once in a while for a two-week stay." She leaned across the table toward me. "They say that there's a plastic surgeon who lives on the premises. I heard that Natasha Forrest checked in at Aphrodite's with a thirty-two-inch bustline and left with a thirty-six." She smiled down at her décolletage, which displayed the source of her smugness. "You notice that right after that, she started wearing low-cut gowns on TV."

"They get movie people and TV celebrities there, eh?" Jerry asked.

"And jet setters, too," Aunt Ceil said, warming to her favorite topic: gossip. "Bobbie Blair, Bibi Fenster . . . they all go there."

"Well, I'm not going there," my dad said, "but I am

going to my office tomorrow. And Linda has an early meeting about her group raising funds for Children's Hospital of Orange." He turned to Mom. "Are you about ready to roll, Linda?"

"Anytime, dear," Mom answered.

We all got up from the table and made our way toward the foyer.

"Aren't you going to stay for just a little while?" I asked.

"We stayed a long time," Aunt Ceil said, "but most of it was spent waiting."

"I'm sorry about that, Mrs. Fein," Dave Rose said. "But *The Register* won't run itself. And Jerry is on call anytime something breaks on the crime front. You should have eaten without us."

"Exactly what *I* said," Aunt Ceil responded, "but I was voted down." She stood posing while Bruno draped a mink cape over her shoulders. Not that she needed to wear it—the evening wasn't that chilly. But Ceil had known she was coming to Harry's house for dinner. And she's the type who gets up in the middle of the night to go to the john but puts on makeup before she goes. She turned to me before she went out the door. "Do look into Aphrodite's, Doris," she said. "I want to know what the inside of the place looks like. I've heard so much."

"And I've heard enough about losing weight," Uncle Saul said, taking her firmly by the elbow. "You almost spoiled my second helpings and dessert."

Mom and Dad left after we exchanged kisses. Because Dad had taken a few scotches before, and a brandy after dinner, Mom was driving. She doesn't drink. Just as he went out the door, Dad whispered to me, "Don't let Ceil get to you, Dee-Dee. I love all of you."

"Sorry about the lateness, Doris," Dave said as he and Jerry were leaving.

"No need, I understand."

"A lovely meal, Ms. Fein, and a lovely hostess," Jerry Kobrin said. "If the dinners come with the job on *The Register*, I'll never want to leave Santa Amelia." And with this, he kissed my hand. It tickled. The beard, you know.

"C'mon, Mr. Suave," called Dave Rose from the driveway. He intentionally mispronounced it *swayve*. "Or you walk home."

"Coming, coming," he grumbled, and to me he said with a grin, "The man's a slavedriver. A regular Simon Levine."

I closed the door and left Bruno to straighten up the house. Not that he would have accepted help. He would have been scandalized, I think. But it's hard to tell what Bruno thinks. He doesn't communicate. He just *does* things without a word. I walked up the elaborate staircase to the second floor of the big old house.

I should have been cheered by Daddy's parting whispered remark to me. I wasn't. He was saying that fat or thin, he loved me. But to say it *that* way: "I love *all* of you." It somehow made me sad.

I paused at the landing above the foyer and looked down. The great staircase, with its highly polished mahogany banisters, gave me a bird's-eye view of the foyer below. A sudden thought crossed my mind. I looked over at the open doors to the dining room. Bruno was nowhere in sight.

On an impulse, I swung one leg over the banister and with a whoop of glee slid down its length to the foyer. I miscalculated my rate of acceleration. I zipped right by the end of the banister and landed with a thud on the black and white marble floor. Fortunately, where I landed, I was best padded.

I was on my hands and knees getting up when I saw two highly polished shoes approach me. I looked up and saw Bruno.

"Did you call, Ms. Fein?" he asked.

I felt a rush of red come to my cheeks. Then I suddenly remembered that it was my house, not Bruno's. And if I wanted to slide down the banisters, well, they were my banisters. I got to my feet, ignoring Bruno's extended hand, and defiantly looked him in the eye.

"No, Bruno. I didn't call. I whooped. I was sliding down the banister and I whooped!" Then, with as much dignity as I could muster under the circumstances, I walked slowly up the stairs. I resisted the temptation to rub my sore bottom until I was sure Bruno had enough time to get back to the dining room. When I got to the top of the landing, I did give in and rub.

"Good night, Ms. Fein," came Bruno's voice from the foyer. Darn him! He had the last word, after all.

3/ *Shirley Is a Grand Old Name*

The old Burroughs Estate is situated only five minutes away from Harry's house. I call it the Burroughs Estate because everyone else in Santa Amelia does. The Burroughs family was one of the first settlers of Santa Amelia. United States settlers, of course. The Spanish had a mission here, and before them, there were the Native Americans. But the house hasn't been owned by the Burroughs family in years.

There was some publicity in the papers when Aphrodite's first opened five years ago, but that soon died down. I'd wondered about that, but last night, at dinner, I'd found out it was because of its policy of confidentiality. I guess no movie star or TV personality wants it known that her beauty is fading. Or that she is getting fat and old.

I'd often imagined what it must be like to receive the pampering and special treatment that jet setters and the like got at Aphrodite's. Now I was going to find out.

I guided the Gumdrop up the winding drive to the main building, which is quite elegant. Along the way, peeking through the carefully manicured landscaping, I caught glimpses of the individual bungalows that dot the three and a half acres of grounds.

As I pulled up in front of the main building, a liveried attendant materialized from inside the house. Don't get me wrong. I don't mean liveried in the East Coast or European sense. The young man wasn't wearing a uniform greatcoat with braid and a cap with visor. He was liveried in the Southern California sense. He wore a pale blue short-sleeved tunic with the Aphrodite logo on the breast pocket, matching slacks, and tennis shoes. The logo, in case you've never seen it, is the silhouette of an impossibly well-built woman against a water-spray background. One assumes the water spray represents the Fountain of Youth. Or maybe Perrier.

The attendant came around and I think was going to open the driver's side door of the Gumdrop for me. Can you imagine? I quickly opened my own door and rolled my bulk out.

"You must be Miss Doris," the attendant said. He was in his twenties, I should judge. *Verry* handsome and muscular, with dark hair, pale blue eyes, and the ubiquitous California tan. This being November, I'm sure he had to work hard to get the color.

"How did you know who I was?" I asked. "Were you warned to look for someone who fit too well in a TR-7?"

He laughed. "Not at all," he said in a well-modulated voice that betrayed an accent I couldn't quite place. "Yours was the only appointment today. Miss Shirley said to be on the lookout for you." He put out his hand. "I'm Mario, the masseur."

"How do you do?" I said inanely. What else do you say when someone sticks out a hand that way? I really didn't care how he did. But now I at least knew *what* he did. To my annoyance, he gave my hand a little squeeze. Not a bone cruncher, but one of those snide, let's-get-together-later squeezes.

I've met guys like him before. They're so caught up with their own good looks that they make overtures to strange women automatically. Then they stand back, expecting you to swoon at their feet with delight that they noticed you. I was about to say something, but got cut off.

"Right this way, Miss Doris," he said, going toward the house. "Miss Shirley expects you. I'm so glad you're on time. So few California people are."

I ignored the shot at us locals and followed him through the doors of the neo-Georgian facade.

The floor of the foyer was gleaming parquetry, with a central Oriental runner that divided and branched off into doorways off the ground floor. A huge double staircase dominated the foyer and led to the second-floor rooms. We stayed on the ground floor and headed toward the rear of the house.

"She's in the solarium," Mario said over his shoulder as we came to a set of massive oaken doors with French door handles. He knocked, and before anyone would have had a chance to answer, the door opened and Mario nearly collided with a medium man. No, he didn't have a crystal ball under his arm. I mean he was medium in all respects. He was of medium height and weight. He was in his middle years, I'd say about fifty. His hair was medium brown, as were his eyes. His hairline was receding but he was only medium bald. He was the sort of fellow who makes the best sort of secret agent or undercover man. An hour after seeing him, you'd never be able to pick him out of a crowd. He wasn't wearing the Aphrodite livery. He was wearing the buttoned-at-the-throat white smock that is the universal garb of doctors and medical attendants everywhere. He was also wearing a bemused look.

"Uh . . . hello, Mario," the medium medico said. "Aren't you supposed to be watching for . . ." He broke off as he saw me. He arranged his face into a medium warm smile and said, "Ah! You must be Doris Fein. I'm Lucius Keene, the house physician." He gave me a medium firm, dry handshake. European style: one downward shake and release.

"Pleased to meet you," I said. Another inanity. I didn't know if I was pleased or not.

"I was just going out to see if you had arrived," he said.

"I don't know if I'm ready for all this rampant hospitality," I replied. "Is it usual for the house doctor to greet new clients?"

"There you have it," Dr. Keene exclaimed. I almost turned around to see what I had. "You employ the term *usual.* There is no place on earth like Aphrodite's. So what is usual in other places is not usual here."

I felt the way Alice did when Humpty Dumpty explained the word *glory.*

"What I meant," I said, "was that a doctor isn't the sort of person one expects as a greeter." I was rewarded by a vague look from Dr. Keene. I could see I wasn't getting through. "My father is a doctor," I explained, "and he speaks of the dignity of professional men."

"Oh, that," Dr. Keene said airily. "We're very informal here . . . ha-ha-ha." That's how he laughed. He actually said *ha-ha-ha.* Three of them, well pronounced and evenly spaced. It was manufactured jollity. Like a department store Santa going *ho-ho-ho.*

He swung the door wide and made an "after you" gesture. I walked into the room. Dr. Keene dismissed Mario and joined me, closing the door silently behind him.

The room was gorgeous. The furniture was pure Scandinavian, all teak, mahogany, and rosewood. There were rya rugs on the floor, allowing the parquetry to show through in places. The walls were white, not the pale blue color of the halls, which I later learned was called Aphrodite Blue, designed exclusively for this luxury fat farm. On the walls were oils by trendy painters, and here and there a French Impressionist. At the far end of the room was a solarium. Amid the plants was a great slab of a rosewood matched-grain desk. Seated behind it, reading some correspondence, was the most beautiful woman I've ever seen.

She'd evidently heard the near-silent closing of the door. Without looking up, she said, "Is she here yet, Lucius?"

"Um . . . very much so, Miss Shirley," Dr. Lucius replied. The beautiful woman looked up then and saw me. She got up from her desk and came across the room.

She was five feet eight, at least. Perfectly formed and fleshed, a striking redhead, with green eyes and a complexion best described as luminous. She was wearing an unadorned knit dress of Aphrodite Blue. She didn't need any ornaments. The uneventful knit dress showed in detail the perfection of her figure. She walked with that gawky elegance found only in Siamese cats and high-fashion models. At that moment something in my mind clicked.

"Serena!" I cried. "You're Serena!" I should know. All the time I was growing up, my mother was her biggest fan. Ten years ago, you couldn't have picked up a copy of *Vogue, Harper's Bazaar* or any such publication without finding Serena in its pages or on the cover. My mom spent countless hours trying to emulate her hairdos, wear her styles, and generally make herself over in Serena's image. Unfortunately, Linda Fein is five feet three inches tall, has brown hair and eyes, and is a bit short in the leg and bottom heavy. Needless to say, Mom's efforts to resemble Serena didn't quite come off.

"My goodness," said the apparition of beauty, "I wouldn't think one as young as you would know my professional alias. It's been years since I've modeled." She smiled, showing a set of teeth that my Uncle Saul would have given a "10."

She came into the living room part of her office and waved me to a chair. I plumped down into the softness of a white rosewood-trimmed Saarinen. Serena/Shirley did the impossible. She sat down on the low Scandinavian sofa without a wrinkle showing and in one sinuous, fluid motion. Like a silk scarf settling.

"Nowadays, I'm Shirley Redman," she said, flashing me a 200-watt smile. "It's my real name, and I'm more comfortable with it." She laughed a perfect laugh. "I never liked the Serena name. Bob Kreisler of the Kreisler Agency picked it out," she said, mentioning the name of one of the nation's top modeling agencies. "As he explained, who'd want a glamour figure named Shirley?"

"What's wrong with Shirley?" I asked, thinking of my father's sister, my Aunt Shirley. She's no glamour puss, but she's a very attractive woman.

"Today, nothing," Serena answered. "But in the late nineteen-forties and the fifties, when I broke in, the world was full of Shirleys." She saw me raise my eyebrows, I guess, and went on. "Yes, my dear. I *am* that old. On my next birthday, I shall be fifty-two."

"But . . ." I began.

"I don't look it?" she said, smiling. "Of course I don't. If I did, I'd probably lie about my age. Isn't that silly?

"But yes, I was born in the thirties. At that time, Shirley Temple was America's darling. It seems that every child who had the misfortune to be born female in those years was named Shirley. If you doubt it, check out the women my age. You can't throw a rock at a crowd of them without hitting two Shirleys."

I quickly did some mental arithmetic. Aunt Shirley is two years older than Daddy. That makes her fifty. Shirley/Serena was so right that I laughed aloud, then had to explain to her what was so funny.

"You see?" she said, laughing easily. "But now let's get down to your problem. The one that brings you to Aphrodite's. A bit over the mark, I see."

"You're kind," I replied. "You know that commercial that goes 'if you can pinch an inch'? Well, I came here because I can grab a slab!"

She made a sad face. "Don't ever put yourself down, Doris. . . . May I call you Doris?"

"Of course."

"Then you call me Shirley. We don't use last names here at Aphrodite's. It's more informal. And frankly, some of the guests don't care to have their last names known to other guests."

"I've heard about that," I said. "That when someone checks in here, nobody knows about it."

"Quite true, Doris. We offer our guests more than the most up-to-date and safest self-improvement methods. We offer privacy and security."

"I couldn't care less," I said. "In fact, if all your methods work . . ."

"Oh, they do. They do, indeed," said Dr. Lucius from behind me. "We guarantee they work." I looked askance at Shirley Redman.

"That's right, Doris, dear," she confirmed. "We can't charge the fees we do without guaranteed results. If you follow our regimen to the letter, I can say absolutely that you'll walk out our door the woman you've always dreamed of being."

"Well, I always sort of dreamed of being Bo Derek," I said.

Shirley laughed. "Now, *that* we can't do. But we *can*

make you realize the full potential of what you were born with. Stand up, my dear."

I obliged, and Shirley uncoiled herself and rose like a plume of smoke from the sofa. "Stand up straight, now," she admonished as she walked around me.

"I *am* standing up straight," I came back. "It's the fat that's slouching."

"There you go again, Doris. Putting yourself down. Beauty isn't all physical, you know. Beauty . . . glamour is an attitude as well. Look at Fanny Singer," she added, mentioning the pop singer superstar. "She has a good body, but her eyes are set so close together, she's slightly cross-eyed. She has a nose like a bugle and a chin that makes her profile look like a can opener. But she's glamorous."

I admitted that Shirley was right. "But don't forget," I said, "she can act and sing. I don't do any of those things."

"And she can't run a newspaper, or manage her own affairs, as you do," Shirley said firmly.

"But how did you . . .?"

"Doris, dear," Shirley said, "no one gets past the inquiry stage at Aphrodite's without a thorough check of her background. I told you that we can't have just *any- one* as a guest."

"It costs that much?" I asked.

"Dear, dear Doris," said Shirley sadly, "I wasn't talking of money. I was referring to the privacy of our guests. We have an average of one undercover reporter per month trying to get inside these doors."

"Still and all," I persisted, "a thousand dollars per

day, with extras for medication and the like, isn't what I call chopped liver, either."

"Do you really think so?" she responded. "When you consider that our average guest pays that for a hotel in Monaco or Paris?" She shook her head, and the mane of red hair fell perfectly across her brow. "No, we aren't that expensive, basically. But some of our medications, our natural extracts, come from as far as Tibet. Others have to be smuggled out of the countries of their origin. From behind the Iron Curtain."

"And others we have developed ourselves," Dr. Lucius added. "I have a complete laboratory on the premises. Which reminds me. We must give you a full medical workup, should you choose to stay at Aphrodite's."

"You don't have to," I said quickly. "I saw Dr. McDonald in Santa Amelia. I have all my records and charts. They're in my car."

"Um . . . good. Very good," Dr. Lucius said. "But we employ our own methods here at Aphrodite's. Some methods that your . . ."

"Dr. McDonald."

"Um . . . yes. That he might not be aware of."

"Dr. McDonald has one of the highest board ratings in the country," I said defensively. "And in California, there's no doctor with a higher reputation."

"I meant no offense," Dr. Lucius said quickly. "It's just that here we work with substances that your Dr. McDonald wouldn't normally encounter. We must determine possible allergic reactions and such."

"Lucius is a very careful and methodical man," Shirley said, giving Dr. Keene a look I didn't understand. He reddened slightly, a medium red, then fell silent. Shirley continued her tour around Mount Fein.

"Not too bad, Doris," she said reflectively. "You're just a bit out of shape. I see by your application that you wish to lose thirty pounds in the next six weeks."

"That's true," I said. "But Dr. McDonald says that it would take a crash diet to do that."

"Which is why your Dr. McDonald is *practicing* medicine," said Shirley smoothly, "and I am *delivering* beauty. All your physician could give you is a diet, which you may or may not follow. We work differently. We take a holistic approach. We treat not just the body, but the entire person. If it were as simple as dieting, none of us would be here, would we?"

"You're right about that," I said. "I've dieted, on and off, for most of my life." I spread my arms and did a leaden pirouette. "And you see the results."

"I do, indeed," she said. "But don't be discouraged. At Aphrodite's we don't just run you around and pat and pummel various parts of you with machines. We *motivate.* Of course, in your case, there's already motivation."

"How do you know that?" I said.

"Really, Doris," Shirley replied. "You have set a goal of losing thirty pounds in a very short time. That means you are either going to go somewhere at that time and want to make an impression on someone, or someone will be here in Santa Amelia at that time. Whichever it is, I'd say it involved a man."

"Now, you couldn't have found that out by checking

my background," I protested.

"I didn't have to," Shirley replied. "Nine out of ten women who come here are doing it to make an impression on a man. That's their problem, too."

"If that's their motivation, what's wrong with it?"

"It's *all* wrong," she said. "You shouldn't want to be beautiful for others. You should want it for *yourself.* How can you be attractive to others if, inside, you still feel unattractive? I told you that glamour is an attitude. It comes from within. And that's part of how Aphrodite's works. From within, on your attitude toward yourself. And from without, by rigorous diet and exercise." She came over and laid a hand on my shoulder. "For instance, Doris," she said in a confidential tone, "I think that you are a singularly beautiful woman. Inside."

I looked into those impossible green eyes and felt such a rush of warmth and charm that in that instant, I did believe I was all Shirley said. If you've ever run into one of those people who have what they call charisma, you know how I felt. Like she wasn't someone I had known for ten minutes. It was as though she were the best friend I'd ever had. And as though I'd known her all my life. More than that, I wanted very much to show her I was worthy of her belief in me. I made up my mind at that moment.

"I'll sign up," I said.

"Without even inspecting the facilities?" Shirley asked. "I'm sorry, Doris. I can't let you do that. That's not how we operate here. Our reputation is built on three foundations. Integrity, confidentiality, and results. No one is more important than the other."

That clinched it for me. This wonderful, beautiful creature not only believed in me but was looking out for my best interests as well. "Okay," I said. "I'll look at the facility. Then I'll sign up."

4/ I Meet a Movie Star

Puffing, blowing, and sweating, I rounded the last turn on the cinder jogging track. It was the last lap before I would be allowed to return to the main building. As each foot hit the ground, sending its message of pain and exhaustion to my brain, I thought: So much for luxury spas. True, my accommodations at Aphrodite's were luxurious. The hitch was that during my first day, I hadn't even had a chance to enjoy them.

The afternoon before, Shirley had given me the grand tour of Aphrodite's. I saw the indoor tennis courts, the outdoor tennis courts. The outdoor pool, the indoor pool. The sauna, the steambath, and the gym with its gleaming equipment. I'd inspected the clinic and seen the small operating theater. I'd even been shown the laboratory where Dr. Lucius extracted his miracle juice.

He calls the stuff JK-4. Its exact content is ultra-hush-hush, but he told me that it's extracted from the adrenal

41

glands of some small animal that lives on the Russian-Mongolian border. The stuff has to be smuggled out. I'd had my first injection of it this morning. I couldn't say that it did much. Or anything. But Dr. Lucius told me I wouldn't feel any difference for the first few days.

"After all, Doris," he said, "you have lived the way you do, and eaten the wrong foods, for all of your eighteen years. You can't expect one injection to change your entire body chemistry and metabolic rate."

To tell the truth, even if it had, I was in too much pain to notice. I thought of my cheery bedroom in the main building, with its big, beautiful, king-size bed. If this jogging business was intended to help me shed pounds, it was going to work. I knew that if I ever survived the jogging, I'd be too tired to eat.

I made my way to the main building and was about to go to the second floor when I was intercepted by Mario, the masseur.

"Ah, there you are, Miss Doris," he exclaimed.

"That's *Ms.*," I said.

"Forgive me," Mario oiled, "I am not from your country. I learned only that one calls women *Miss* or *Mrs.* This *Ms.* is something new."

"It's new in this country, too, Mario," I replied. "But it's here to stay; you might as well learn it."

"But what does it mean?"

"If a woman uses the title *Miss* or *Mrs.*," I explained, "it tells what her marital status is: *Miss* if she's single or divorced, *Mrs.* if she's married."

"*Oui,* this I know."

"But a man is always *Mister.* No indication whether

he's married or not," I said.

Mario raised his shoulders and spread his arms. "But what possible difference does it make?" he asked. "I know married women who act single. I know single women who act married. I know men who do the same. It doesn't matter what they are called. It is what they *do, n'est-ce pas?*"

I could see that I'd make no headway with Pretty Boy, so I let the matter drop. "Were you looking for me, Mario?" I asked.

"*Oui,* errr, Ms. Doris. You are finished with the jogging?"

"The jogging has nearly finished me."

"*Bon.* Then you must directly go to the sauna."

"Are you mad?" I squeaked. "I'm awash in my own juices as it is!" It was true. My brand-new Aphrodite Blue sweat suit was more sweat than suit at this point. Not that it mattered. There were a dozen of them hanging in the closet of my room. Just opposite the king-size bed I so longed for.

"Not at all, Ms. Doris," Mario replied. "The sauna will stop your muscles from cramping up after your exercise. Afterward, you come to me for massage. Then you may have lunch."

"Lunch? What time is it?"

"Ten forty-five, Ms. Doris," said Mario, consulting a Rolex on his hairy wrist. I groaned. I'd been up since six that morning. Had I stayed overnight at Aphrodite's, I could have slept later. But since I lived just a few minutes' drive down the road, I'd gone home for the night.

Also, I had to clear the heavy expenditure for Aphrodite's with my lawyer, Brian Donnelly. I'd expected some difficulty with him. He's parsimonious with my money. Shirley had said I'd have to stay at Aphrodite's two weeks. The basic bill without the Lucius-juice was fourteen thousand. But Donnelly never turned a hair. Said that anything that contributed toward my health and welfare was fine with him.

U.C.I. was another matter. The one-week Thanksgiving vacation was due, but a two-week stay at Aphrodite's meant missing a week of lectures. Happily, I'm at the top of my classes, and I got permission. Once I explained, that is.

But here it was, my first day. If all of them were to be like this, I'd have preferred two years on Devils Island. I sighed and followed Mario to the sauna.

We passed through the pool area to the site of the hotbox. I noted some of the other guests. There were two of them swimming in the large pool. I gasped and quickly looked over at Mario. They were totally nude!

I guess that despite my world travels—I've been to France, Italy, and England—I'm a bit of a provincial. To see two grown women swimming in the altogether while a young, handsome man strolled by was a bit much. Oh, yes, I know there are nude beaches in France. They're a separate section of most beaches on the Mediterranean. The French call them *plages naturelles,* which means natural beaches. You can see entire families swimming and sunbathing in the raw. In some cases, you wish that the lumpier ones had kept their clothes on.

If Mario had heard my intake of breath, he didn't let

on. I said, "The pool isn't crowded at all, is it?"

"It never is, Ms. Doris," he said, smiling. "We accommodate no more than twenty-five guests at a time. Each has her own schedule for the pool." He pronounced the word *schedule* like the English do: *shed-yule.* "We have only two guests for the pool at once. It's a safety measure. One should never swim alone after exercise. And to have a lifeguard would be *de trop,* no?"

Mario guided me to the anteroom of the sauna. A neat plastic tag adorned one of the hooks on the wall opposite the wooden door to the hotbox. It read: MS. DORIS. The rest of the room was taken up with leather-covered, chrome-legged benches. A huge pile of over-sized Aphrodite Blue towels rested on a similar table in a corner.

"Stay inside only ten minutes, Ms. Doris," Mario said. "Then exit through the other sauna door. It will bring you to the massage room. I will be waiting. You may drop your exercise suit and shoes in the chute over there. Fresh ones will be waiting on the other side of the sauna." He indicated a small swivel panel in the imitation wood paneling. Then he left the room.

I undressed and went into the redwood room. The heat was like a physical blow at first; then I gradually began to relax. After what seemed like only a few seconds, a red light flashed and a buzzer gave an insistent *brrrrp.* I realized then how Mario had expected me to know when ten minutes was up. I wrapped my towel around my steaming corpus and went through the other door. Mario was waiting in the next room.

He wasn't wearing a shirt. No doubt about it, Mario

was a magnificent physical specimen. He was *verry* hairy, though. The only adornment on his chest besides his pelt of fur was a golden chain. Almost hidden in the Black Forest was a *mans fica,* an Italian charm that wards off the evil eye. A lot of Southern Californians wear them, too. But in their case, I think they're used as amulets to ward off poverty.

Mario patted the nearest massage table. "Please take off your towel and climb up here, Ms. Doris," he said.

"Why take off the towel?" I asked.

"Because the table is already covered with towel cloth . . . what do you call it?"

"Terry cloth."

"*Oui,* terry cloth."

I hesitated. There was no doubt that Mario was a one hundred percent masculine man. And here I was, being urged to take off all my clothes. Well, my towel, anyhow, so he could press my flesh. The problem was resolved by Mario himself.

"Perhaps, Ms. Doris," he said with a smile, "you are a little bit *timide . . .* er, shy?"

"Of course not," I said, shedding the towel and quickly hopping up on the table, face down. In an instant, Mario produced one of the small towels I had seen stacked under the table, and draped it across my rear. The towel was only the size of a hand towel, and I thought to myself how inadequate it was to cover the bulk of what it had to cover. From the rear, it probably looked like a postage stamp on a Parker House roll.

But whatever opinion I may have had of Mario, the man had hands like an angel! In a few minutes, every ache and throb began to leave my body. I was really beginning to enjoy the massage when he said, "Turn over, please."

I gulped. Then I thought: You took off the towel in front of him. If you're in for a penny, you're in for a pound. Actually, in for thirty pounds. Think of him as a piece of equipment. Like a massage machine. I flopped over. Again, he materialized another towel, which he spread over the strategic areas. As though in answer to my unasked question, he gazed down at my upper torso and said, "We don't massage there. No muscle tissue."

If I hadn't been pink from the sauna, I was now. All over.

"This is lunch?" I exclaimed in the dining room. The waitress who had just served me nodded. I gazed down at the small salad and lemon wedge with disbelief. It was flanked by two Rye-Krisp crackers and a small paper sauce cup that contained two capsules and a pill. Topped off with a glass of Perrier, the whole lunch took me three minutes.

After lunch, it was back to the gym. If you've ever seen those commercials for health spas, you know what those machines look like. But if you've never been personally involved in the grunting and pain that they deliver, I can offer a word of advice. *Don't!*

I spent the time under the watchful eye of a lady who had a build that made me look like a guy. She was relentlessly cheerful, a smiling Torquemada who spoke exclusively in first person plural.

"Well, how are we doing with the leg presses, Doris?"
Or "Let's get our legs up a bit higher, Doris."

After fifteen minutes of this, I finally grunted, "When
we die from this, will we be buried together?" She only
laughed and inflicted more torture on me. Then sent
me to swim a hundred yards in the pool. I didn't mind
the no-bathing-suit. I was beyond caring.

I entered the water like Moby Dick collapsing and
nearly collided with another guest who was methodi-
cally swimming the length of the pool, lap after lap.

It was depressing. The woman was gorgeous and
seemed in no more need of the facilities of Aphrodite's
than I needed another twenty pounds.

"Sorry," I said as we surfaced after our near-collision.
"I didn't see you."

"Perfectly all right," she answered, standing up
alongside me in the shallow end. I looked at her slim
but magnificently proportioned body with undisguised
envy. She took off the one article of clothing she was
wearing, a bathing cap, and extended her hand.

"I'm Louise," she said, smiling.

Once she shook out the mane of hair from under the
cap, she didn't have to introduce herself. I recognized
her immediately. I'd seen enough of her films. She was
Louise Sorelle. Actress, society figure, and, on TV, sales-
person for a *verry* expensive line of perfume.

"Why you're . . ." I began.

She put a finger to her lips. "No last names at Aphrodite's, uh . . ."

"Doris. Doris Fei . . . uh, I'm Doris," I replied almost
making the same gaffe.

"Glad to know you, Doris," she said, pronouncing my name like my Uncle Claude does, *Doh-ree.*

Maybe I'm celebrity gaga. I was so caught up in her perfect beauty that I suddenly realized I hadn't let go of her hand. I quickly disengaged. It's odd, but no matter how often you see a celebrity in public or on film, it doesn't prepare you for meeting one in the flesh. In this case, "in the flesh" took on new meaning. I tried to think of all the things I'd want to say to or ask of Louise Sorelle. My mind went blank. Instead of being charming, continental, or witty, I blurted out, "What are you doing here?"

"Why, the same as you, Doh-ree. I am trying to become beautiful."

"But, you, of all people!" I persisted. "You don't need it!"

She laughed. *"Mais certainement,* I need it. Beauty is a full-time employment, Doh-ree. I am—how does one say it?—protecting my investment. In a way, I am a slave to this," she said, indicating the body I would have given everything to live in.

"Then this is a regular thing with you?" I asked.

"Oh, yes, I come here twice each year, for a week's stay. And once a month, I fly in to have some of Dr. Lucius's wonderful JK-4. It keeps one young, you know."

In truth, I didn't know. That part of the JK-4 shots hadn't been stressed during Dr. Lucius's guided tour. But then why should it have? I'm *already* young. But I did some quick mental arithmetic. Louise Sorelle had been a glamorous leading lady for as long as I could recall. She was surely in her middle thirties. But here she was, magnificent bod and all, no makeup, and of course no clothes to hide defects or sags. She was stunningly beautiful.

"And you owe it all to Dr. Lucius's shots?" I asked.

"No, not completely," she admitted. "I am careful about my diet. I take regular exercise. But when one reaches a certain age, the body undergoes changes. After that age, the body's powers to regenerate begin to dwindle. Dr. Lucius's injections restore that ability."

She looked at the cap in her hand. "I must swim another five hundred meters," she said. "No matter. I must shampoo again today." She tossed the cap to one side of the pool and began to swim toward the far end in a steady, strong, measured stroke. I watched that perfect body flashing in the water and eased myself after her.

I'm a good swimmer. My exercise schedule called for only a hundred yards. Tired as I was, Louise Sorelle had provided me with an incentive. I swam five hundred yards before it was time for dinner. Once I got to it, I wondered if it had been worth it. A single lamb chop with no seasoning and, again, a small salad and the pill cup.

I don't know how I made it to the second floor of the main building that night. Actually, it wasn't really nighttime, but it was getting dark outside. The antique grandfather clock on the second-floor landing read 7:00 P.M. The new round of torture would begin promptly at eight tomorrow after breakfast, or whatever the sadist in the kitchen prepared. I knew I wouldn't hear the twin speakers built into the headboard of my bed.

The day before, Shirley had explained about those speakers. It's a form of hypnotherapy that Aphrodite's uses. Before you go to sleep, your weight on the bed activates a tape recording that plays at a level almost below your ability to hear. Shirley had turned up the volume a bit for me, so I could hear what it was saying. Against a background of ocean surf sounds, a voice says to you: *I am beautiful. I am a good person. I will be beautiful inside and outside. I am a good person. I am a worthwhile human being. . . .*

You get the idea. I'm familiar with the concept. A variation on it was used by the Russians during the cold war. For brainwashing. In this case, it was being put to constructive use.

But tonight, I was so whipped by the exercise, sauna, and massage that I knew I'd be asleep before my head hit the pillow. Not that it matters. I understand from Shirley that the suggestion system works even when you're asleep.

I went into my room. I debated with myself whether or not to bathe before going to bed. I felt waterlogged as it was. I'd had three showers, a sauna, and a swim already. The oversized bed loomed invitingly. I thought to myself, I should brush my teeth. Then answered myself: What for? You hardly had anything to eat!

My dog-tired body resolved it. Without shedding my Aphrodite blue sweat suit, my third that day, I flopped face downward across the huge bed. I hadn't even turned off the lights. As I lay there in utter exhaustion,

I could hear the tape begin to play from the headboard speakers.

I am beautiful. . . .

"I am bushed," I replied into the mattress.

I am a good person. . . .

"I am a good and tired person."

I will be beautiful, inside and outside. . . .

"I will be tortured inside and jogged to death outside."

I am a good person. . . .

"I am an almost dead person."

I felt a strange sensation spreading across the lower front of my sweat suit. Warm, but not warm. Fluid and sticky. What in the world . . . ? I stood up and looked down. A red stain, thick and syrupy, was spread across my lower body. There was a huge red stain on the bedsheets.

"I'm bleeding to death!" I screamed.

5/ Kinky for Pies

"Will you be quiet?" came a voice from behind me. "You'll have the whole staff up here in a minute!"

I turned around, and standing in my doorway was a plumpish woman with blond hair. She was in her late thirties, I'd guess. She was wearing an Aphrodite sweat suit and a look of anguish.

"Oh, no!" she exclaimed, rushing to the bloodied bed. "You ruined it. You squished it all up!"

"I'm bleeding to death, and you're talking about a bed!" I yelled at her. "Do something! Get Dr. Lucius. I'm bleeding, can't you see?" To my amazement, this loony lady began to laugh.

"It hurts me more than it does you," she said. She went to the bloodstained bed and whipped back the pale blue sheets. "Look at the cause of your 'hemorrhage.'"

I looked and nearly collapsed from relief. There, in the center of the bed, was the source of the gore. She rushed over to it like a mother to a wounded child.

"A perfectly good cherry pie," she groaned, "and you've ruined it beyond repair!" She prodded the pan-caked pastry with a forefinger and put the carmined finger in her mouth. "Tastes okay, though. Lucky you didn't pull the sheet back before you squished it. It's okay to eat, still. Care to join me?"

I regarded the woman with wonder. She picked up a relatively unmashed section of the cherry pie and popped it into her mouth. Then she wiped her hand on the side of her sweat suit and extended the now-sticky hand to me.

"I'm Katy Byrd," she said, "your next-door neighbor. Sorry about the pie. I thought the room was empty. Nobody told me that we have a new victim here. I better check the rest of my stash."

She began going through the room, and from each nook and drawer she produced something else to eat. "Just gathering up the goodies," she said over her shoul-der as she disappeared into my closet. She emerged with two boxes of Twinkies. She added them to the growing stack of comestibles on the gory bed. There were candy bars, barbecue chips, beef jerky, and who knows what other varieties of junk food by the time she was finished.

"There, that's the lot," she said, sitting down on my bed and peeling the wrapper off a Milky Way. Immedi-ately, the bed began to intone: *I am beautiful.* . . .

"Ahh, shaddup!" Katy Byrd said to the bed and reached over behind the headboard. She grabbed something and yanked. *I am a good wrrrk!* said the speakers, and expired. She turned triumphantly with a piece of blue-coated wire in her hand.

"Talky damn thing," she said. "Anything I can't stand, it's a gabby bed. I had a husband . . . I think he was the third one. Used to talk in bed all the time. Drove me nuts. I figure if you're in bed, it's to sleep, or whatever. No need for conversation in either case."

I gazed at Katy Byrd, munching away at her candy bar. Then I looked down at myself, with cherry pie all over me. I guess it was a combination of relief to know I wasn't dying and the stress of the day's activities. I began to roar with laughter. Katy joined in. I was weak from laughing, and without thinking, sat down heavily alongside her. Smack on the remains of the flattened cherry pie.

"Hey, don't do that!" Katy Byrd protested. "I've heard of kinky, but anyone who sits on cherry pies is *really* strange!"

That night was the beginning of a warm friendship between Katy Byrd and me. Katy broke all the rules of Aphrodite's and kept coming up smiling. The rules she couldn't change were our seating arrangements at meals and our swimming time. But she tried.

"It's part of the Aphrodite plan to get you psyched up to lose weight," she explained to me the second night of my stay. "They pair a fatty with a glamour puss. The fatty feels incentive to look like the skinny. The fatty scares the skinny one into staying that way."

"I'd say it was pretty clever," I said, recalling the way I'd felt when swimming with Louise Sorelle. And still did, if it came to that.

Katy Byrd waved a hand disparagingly. "Cheap living-room psychology," she said. "You can't be manipulated if you know where the strings are being pulled. It's like aversion therapy: a cheap shot."

"You mean, like they scare people out of smoking cigarettes with shots of what cancer does to you?"

"Exactly," Katy said. "Except the bulk of people who smoke aren't smoking for reasons that are affected by scare tactics. It's deep-seated, and a few horror movies won't change it."

"Then why do you come here at all?" I asked. "You don't believe in their system. And you break all their rules. Like you told me your last name as soon as we met."

"Names!" she said in disgust. "I've had five husbands. I've changed my name so often, my towels don't say *His* and *Hers.* They're marked: *To Whom It May Concern.*" She peeled the wrapper off a Twinkie.

"I come here because it's *the* place to come," she went on. "If you're in a social circle where everyone has a Rolls or a Mercedes, and everyone has a showplace home, what's your one-up? Travel? No, anyone with a credit card can go to Cannes. Pal around with actors? Silly. Have you ever spent any time talking to actors?"

"Not really."

"They talk about two things. Their last role and themselves. Then, when your eyes start to glaze over, they look you in the eye and say, 'But enough about me. What did *you* think of my performance?' "

"I get the idea."

"So I come to this place," Katy continued. "It does

work, if you keep the rules. I've lost seven pounds in the past two weeks. And all the time, I've been eating in my room."

"How do you get all this stuff?" I asked.

"I go out and buy it, of course," Katy Byrd said. "This is a spa, not a jail. You can go out if you want. I hop into my Jaguar and tootle into town. I load up the trunk and come back. That simple."

"But isn't it self-defeating?"

"What if it is? It's my money. If I want to spend a thousand a day, I can afford it. It's worth it just to gossip about who was here when I get back to San Francisco."

"But the privacy Shirley talked about . . ."

"A lot of bull," Katy sneered. "It's the most beautiful and subtle advertising campaign in the world. It doesn't cost her a dime, and the Aphrodite name is dropped where it can do her the most good."

"Makes sense," I said.

"And dollars," Katy added. "Real big bucks. Do you realize that with twenty-five guests, the basic weekly income here is a hundred seventy-five thousand dollars? And that's without Lucius Keene's monkey-gland extract shots. They go for two hundred fifty bucks a pop, and you get two a day."

"I started trying to figure out how much the spa grossed annually," I admitted, "but with all the extras, I lost count."

"Try multiplying your wildest guess by five times, and you'll be close," Katy Byrd said. "And naturally, Shirley and Lucius aren't putting the dough under their mattresses. They've got every cent out earning for them. You could say that they're living off the fat of the land."

"And living well," I added. I sat down on my bed, checking to make sure Katy hadn't hidden anything else in it. Immediately, the bed began to talk: *I am beautiful. . . .*

"They fixed it," I said, getting up.

"Naturally," Katy said. "Can't allow you to sleep without the inspirational messages. First week I was here, they fixed it six times. After that, they got *my* message and didn't bother anymore."

"But they don't throw you out," I said.

"Throw me out?" Katy hooted. "I'm one of their best customers! I've been coming here since the first year they opened. I've seen all the biggies come and go. Louise is a regular, Fanny Singer, Bobbie Blair . . ."

"Fanny Singer comes here?" I said in wonder.

"Four weeks a year," Katy said, nodding. "You'd think after all this time, Lucius would have talked her into a nose job."

"But her profile is her trademark," I protested.

"You talk like she's got a choice," Katy snorted. "I was kidding. Have you any idea what she'd look like with a small nose? Her eyes are so close together, she'd look like a flounder. Both eyes on the same side of her face."

I had to laugh at the idea. "But I didn't know Dr. Lucius was a plastic surgeon," I said. "I thought he was some sort of biologist, with his extracts and all."

"Oh, luscious Lucius is a jack of all trades. If you want a nose job, a face lift, a tummy tuck . . . ."

"What's a tummy tuck?" I asked.

"Poor baby," Katy cooed, "you've led a sheltered life. They open up a flap of skin on your abdomen and remove the fatty tissue underneath. Then they close you up, and *voilà!* A flat tummy without a hundred situps a day."

"That sounds like major surgery to me," I said.

"It is," Katy replied. "Lucius has a whole cadre of surgical assistants. When he knows he's got someone coming in for plastic surgery, he flies in the extra help from Ohio."

"Why Ohio?" I asked.

"Why not?" countered Katy. "I think Lucius is originally from Ohio. Shaker Heights or some such place."

I stood up and turned down my bed. Then I went into the bathroom and started my nightly tub. I missed my baths at Harry's mansion. Funny how you can get used to something absolutely luxurious so fast. Over the roar of the water, Katy called to me, "Think I'll turn in, too. Got a big day tomorrow. Five laps around the track, and then into Santa Amelia for a Big Mac and a side of fries."

"Well, I'm going to stick with the rules," I said, coming back into the bedroom. "I had my weight checked tonight. I lost three entire pounds yesterday."

"Just fluid loss," Katy said. "Between the sauna and running around, you drop a lot in the first few days. Then the real hard work starts. I did the only sensible thing."

"Which is?"

"I gave up."

I said my good-nights, took my bath, and settled down into my chatterbox bed. The day's activities had me utterly worn out.

I am beautiful, said my bed. . . .

"Please, Ms. Fein," the photographer begged, "just one more shot?"

"Ms. Fein is very busy," my manager said brusquely. "We have a motion picture to shoot."

"Clear the set!" the assistant director called. "All you media people. Out!"

The director approached me. "In this scene, Doris baby, you are very sad. Your lover has left you for a sweet, simple girl from Ohio. Your millions mean nothing to you. You open a bottle of champagne. . . . Then you take the pills. . . . You take off your robe and, in your bikini, slowly walk down the steps into the swimming pool. We'll shoot the American version for TV first. Then you'll do it again without the bikini, okay?"

"Gotcha," I said.

"Makeup!" called the director. "Check her out!"

"What for?" said my makeup lady. "Her eyes are fine, and she doesn't need any makeup."

"Speed!" someone called. The sound was being recorded now. I slipped off my robe as the camera dollied in.

"Wow, what a bod!" I heard a grip whisper.

"Cut!" screamed the director. "I said it had to be quiet on the set. Haven't you guys seen enough women in bathing suits?"

"Not with a body like that!" came a voice from the light galleries above us. A long, low whistle followed. The director grinned.

"Sorry, Doris baby," he said. "It's the price of being a sex symbol. . . . Now can we get to work?"

"Ready when you are, C.B.," I said.

I went through the scene without a hitch. The director called "Cut!" and we set up for the next.

"Now, this is where your lover comes back and finds you in the pool. He's changed his mind. He's so fascinated by you that he had to come back. He sees you in the pool. . . . He screams your name. Then he dives in, fully clothed, and pulls you out. Now, remember, you have to be perfectly limp."

"I know, I know," I said. "But make sure he gets into the water fast enough. I can't float face down forever."

"Just take a very deep breath," the director said.

"That I really want to see," I heard someone say.

The scene began. I held my breath. I felt and heard the splash as my leading man entered the pool. I felt strong arms pick me up and carry me out of the pool. My eyes were shut tight.

"Darling, darling! Speak to me!" I heard a familiar voice say. I opened my eyes and there, holding me in his arms, was Larry Small!

"Thank God you're alive!" he said. "I have something for you."

He reached behind him, and then before I knew what was happening, he hit me square in the face with a cherry pie!

.   .   .

I sat up in bed with a start. A second later, my alarm rang, and the ever-present taped music began to come from the speakers in my headboard. There's canned music all through the spa. It's their one big lapse in taste. It's all that syrupy violins-and-slush stuff you hear in elevators. I think they were playing "Home on the Range." As a tango. I got up and steeled myself for the ordeal that lay ahead.

Katy Byrd could say what she liked, but the Aphrodite plan began to work. Over the next ten days, the fat seemed to melt away. After the first week, I guess my stomach shrank. I no longer had any desire to eat. My muscle tone began to improve. I no longer was panting at the end of my morning jogging sessions. I was up to a thousand yards a day at my pool time. Louise Sorelle had left at the beginning of the second week. And you can imagine my satisfaction when, after two days with an equally devastating swim partner, my schedule was changed. My new partner was a lady of fifty named Monica. She outweighed me by easily twenty-five pounds. My heart sang. I was now the thin, graceful ideal *she* was inspired by!

The world was a happy place. I was getting thinner by the day. Shirley Redman was a wonderful person. Dr. Lucius was the best doctor in the world. Next to Dr. Lucius, Marcus Welby was a surly old curmudgeon. I was almost devastated when Shirley called me into her office the day before I was due to leave.

I'd been hoping she would ask me to stay on. I loved the place. Even Mario seemed sweet and charming.

Shirley inspected my progress chart with open satisfaction. I glowed.

"You've done beautifully, Doris," she said with a smile that warmed my soul. "You have lost eighteen pounds in two weeks. But more important, you have gained the sense of well-being that marks all of our Aphrodite guests. You are beautiful. Inside and out."

She looked through more of my charts. Then she got up and walked around her desk to where I stood. She put her arms around me.

"I'm so very proud of you, Doris," she said. "And I know that you'll stay with your regimen. I realize that you must get back to your classes at U.C.I. But since you live down the road, you can make full use of our facilities any time you choose. If you like, I can set up an exercise schedule that accommodates your program at school."

"I'd love it!" I cried.

"Very well, Doris," Shirley said. "You will, of course, continue to come here to Dr. Lucius for your JK-4 injections. They must continue. I'm afraid that even once you're at your ideal weight, you'll have to have them at least once a month to control your new metabolism."

"No problem," I said brightly. "I'll be right down the road. I have a sauna of my own. But no masseur."

"Mario could possibly make a house call, seeing that you *do* live so near," Shirley said reflectively. "But this can't be known to any of the other guests. I pay Mario very well. Any one of my guests would try to hire him away from me if they knew."

"I'll be silent as the grave," I promised. I took Shirley's hand. "I just want you to know that I appreciate what you've done for me," I said.

"Nonsense!" Shirley replied. *"You* did it. We provided the facilities, that's all. I must admit that Dr. Lucius's discovery has a great deal to do with it, though. JK-4 is remarkable stuff. That's why you must continue with your shots, Doris. And now you can go home. If you continue the regimen planned for you, the other twelve pounds will be gone by the time your young man gets to town." I left the office walking on air, with a springy, muscular step.

I went upstairs to get my street clothes. I was hoping to see Katy Byrd, but she was off somewhere, probably jogging while eating a Clark bar. I left her a note. As I did, I suddenly realized that if Katy Byrd left Aphrodite's, I wouldn't know how to reach her, and I didn't want to lose track of her. All I knew about where she lived was a passing reference she had made to San Francisco. I asked her in my note to send her address to me.

The next three weeks, I kept firmly to my original schedule. I even added a few new wrinkles of my own. Instead of jogging alone, I took the Rover Boys with me, running around the grounds of the big estate. They loved the exercise. With each passing day, I began to feel better and better. And each time I got on the beam scale I'd bought for the bathroom, I felt better yet.

I guess the high point was when I went to Fashion Island in Newport Beach. It's a monstrous shopping center, dedicated to the proposition that all Californians aren't equal—financially. They have a branch of Neiman Marcus there, for openers.

After that I went to the other big Orange County center, South Coast Plaza, and raided I. Magnin and Saks Fifth Avenue. By the time I was done, I had an entire new wardrobe. Extravagant, you say? Not at all. I needed it. Not one article of my old wardrobe fit me anymore. It was all too big!

I hadn't realized how skinny I'd been getting until after seeing Dr. Lucius my second week as an outpatient. While there I visited a bit with Katy Byrd.

"Doris, you're skinny as a rail!" she chortled. "You make me want to follow the rules. Well, almost."

"But you look good yourself," I replied. It was true. Despite all her flaunting of the regulations, the exercise, diet, and shots were working. Katy had shed inches.

"Outside of the gossip, it's another reason I keep coming back," Katy admitted. "I may break the rules, but even with doing that, I'm taking on less than I do at home. Oh, by the way . . ."

She rummaged in her purse, and after taking out two small fruit pies from McDonald's and a candy bar, she produced a calling card.

"Here's my address in San Francisco. Anytime you're in town, pop in on me. If I'm in town, that is." She laughed. "What a hoot," she said. "I'm *always* in town. My last husband was a compulsive traveler. I've taken every damn excursion flight, cruise, and hiking tour there is. I forgot what my house looked like after a while."

"It doesn't sound all that bad," I said. "I love to travel myself."

"It's a bug, like the flu," Katy said. "Once you've weathered it, you become immune. But some people never get over it. Like Bobbie Blair."

"You know Bobbie Blair?" I asked. I was curious about her. She had sort of typified the jet set for some years.

"Know her?" said Katy. "We're bosom buddies. In a real sense. We both had breast implants done here." Katy patted her ample bosom.

"Bobbie Blair had implants?" I squeaked. "I thought her figure was so perfect."

"She's plastic from the collarbones down, honey," Katy Byrd said. "Same as me. I wonder what's become of her, though. I haven't seen her or heard from her in a year. . . . Saw her here, then. That was when she became too exclusive for any of her old pals. I hear she's living in South America somewhere. Little stinker. I got one postcard from Rio, and that was it." Her face brightened. "But you do look great, honey. Best of luck when Larry Small gets to town."

I had confided to Katy my motive for being at Aphrodite's. We promised to see each other again as soon as we had time. Probably over the holidays.

I had just left Katy's room when I ran into Shirley coming down the corridor.

"Why, Doris, what a lovely surprise!" she said. "What brings you upstairs? Lonely for your old room?"

"Just visiting with Katy Byrd," I said.

"Please, no last names," said Shirley, frowning. "Katy

is a problem. She feels rules are for others, not her."

"But she's great fun," I said. "I've never met anyone like her. She knows everyone and has a choice tidbit of gossip about each person she knows. From Fanny Singer to Bobbie Blair."

"What did she say about Bobbie?" Shirley looked startled.

I debated whether or not I should tell her. But I have this thing about lying. Once you start, it's a downhill course.

"Katy told me about the breast implant," I said. "But you can trust me, Shirley. My lips are sealed. I'd no more tell anyone about Bobbie Blair than I would about Katy. I *do* believe in the rules." I pirouetted in front of her. "Look what the rules have done for me!"

"Did she say anything else about Bobbie?" Shirley persisted.

"Not a thing," I replied. "Just that she hasn't seen her since last year. That's all."

Shirley looked visibly relieved. "Really, I must have a talk with Katy," she said.

"Don't get me in trouble, now," I said.

"I wouldn't dream of it, Doris, dear," Shirley said. "Now, have you seen Dr. Lucius yet?"

"Just on my way," I said, leaving.

I stopped at the landing and glanced back down the hall. I had expected to see Shirley go into Katy's room. But she didn't. She went to an intercom phone that hung on the corridor wall. As I left the landing, I could barely hear her say, "Hello . . . Lucius?"

6/ Can This Be Larry Small?

I'm not quite sure what I expected Larry Small to do when he saw the new me. I stood at the terminal gate at John Wayne Airport where he couldn't miss me as he deplaned. I was wearing my very first pair of designer jeans and a western-cut shirt with a scarf at the neck. I'd had my hair styled shorter than I usually wear it and, I must confess, it was two shades lighter. I couldn't bring myself to wear cowboy boots, but I wore boot-cut shoes. The whole ensemble was topped off with a pearl-gray Stetson hat with a low crown.

The AirCal flight pulled in and passengers began entering the terminal. I fidgeted a bit. I knew I looked good. Before I'd sprayed my designer jeans on, I had checked myself out in the full-length mirror. I'd seen something I'd never seen in my life. My hip bones!

I almost missed seeing Larry. I was expecting to see the same Larry Small I had last seen in Santa Amelia, before he'd gone to work for the magazine in San Fran-

68

cisco. I wasn't prepared for the *man* who got off the plane.

He didn't look like what you'd think a *Rolling Stone* critic should look like. He had his hair cut quite short. To make up for it, he sported a well-trimmed beard. He wore a three-piece suit of navy blue and a pale blue shirt with a red striped tie. A raincoat (an absolute necessity in San Francisco's dank winters) hung over one arm. And so help me, he had an attaché case in the other hand! I called out his name, and he looked straight at me before he recognized me.

"Doris?" he said tentatively. "Is that you?"

"I was going to ask you the same question," I replied. Before I could say another word, he had dropped both briefcase and coat and planted a big wet one on my lips, with accompanying bear hug. Then he held me at arm's length and said, "Dee, you look wonderful! My gosh, what have you done to yourself?"

"Just taking care of business," I said airily.

"Later for show business," he said. *"Your* business is just beautiful. And so are you. Tell me, what happened? What did you do to yourself? How did . . . "

I precluded further conversation by returning the kiss I'd been given. "Later," I said. "We can talk on the way to Santa Amelia. I have the car at a parking meter. Do you have any other luggage?"

"Yeah, just a couple of suitcases."

"You go ahead and get them," I said. "I'll put another dime in the infernal machine. See you at the baggage claim." I began to walk toward the parking area, when Larry called out to me. I turned. He was standing there grinning like a cat with feathers in his mouth.

"Yes?" I called.

"Nothing, Dee," he said, smiling. "Just that you look good walking away, too." I was airborne to the parking lot. I fed the one-armed bandit a dime and hotfooted it back to the terminal. Just as Larry was coming out the main gates with suitcases, I grabbed one.

"Take the attaché case, Doris," he said. "The suitcases are kinda heavy."

It was showing off, I know, but I had to do it. I had spent so much time at Aphrodite's heaving chromed levers and weights about, the suitcase felt like nothing at all. I picked it up with one hand and, with a grin, did two curls. That's when you lift a weight and, using only your forearm, pull the weight toward you.

"I don't know what you're talking about, Larry Small," I said. "It's light as a feather." The look on Larry's face was worth at least two of the puffing-and-pain sessions I'd spent at the gym.

We levered Larry's luggage into the trunk of the Gumdrop and behind the seats. Larry looked over the TR-7.

"Still with the Gumdrop, hey?" he said. "I thought by now you'd be driving a Porsche or a Mercedes."

"I have a perfectly good car of my own. One I bought with my own money," I said. "I have two other cars at Harry's place. But I thought picking you up in a Mercedes 600 limousine would be a bit much. And I'm not quite sure how the other car works."

"You're kidding," Larry said, getting into the Gumdrop. "What kind of car is it?"

"A model 316 Cord Phaeton," I said, starting up the engine.

"A what?" Larry gulped.

"You heard it," I answered, easing out of the parking lot and into the traffic on MacArthur Boulevard. "A 1936 Cord. It's got some funny kind of gear-shift thingie on the steering column."

"A preselector," Larry said in awe. "It's a preselector."

"Whatever," I said, and we were off for home. Larry's, that is. His mom hadn't been able to get to the airport to meet him. She's a nurse at Pacifica Hospital, and her hours change constantly.

All through the fifteen-minute drive to Santa Amelia, Larry kept looking over at me. I was concentrating on the traffic, which was heavy. Larry had arrived in the teeth of the rush hour. Don't laugh. We have a very heavy rush hour in Orange County. The area has grown so in the past few years that trying to get to Santa Amelia from John Wayne Airport at rush hour is like trying to get to Orange County from Los Angeles at 5:00 P.M.

I took streets, not freeways. Even so, it was stop and go most of the way. I caught Larry staring at me as I checked traffic at an intersection.

"Something?" I asked.

"I can't get over it, Dee," he said, shaking his head. "It's as though you're a completely different person. But when you talk, you're the same Doris."

"I should hope so," I said, avoiding a tractor trailer that seemed intent on mashing us into Harbor Boulevard. "I spent a lot of time and effort working on the outside of me. But I wasn't dissatisfied with me inside to begin with."

"What do your folks think of the new house?" Larry asked. "They get used to it yet?"

"They're not living with me, Larry," I replied. "Dad wouldn't move."

"For Pete's sake, why not?"

"He says that he worked too long for the house on Oak Street to give it up. He's proud of what he's done. And I agree with him. I would have gotten my own place my sophomore year at U.C.I. anyhow." Larry laughed.

"What's the big joke?" I asked.

"It gives new meaning to me saying, 'My place or yours?' that's all."

"Don't get any ideas, Larry Small," I said. "Bruno stayed on at Harry's place, and he's *verry* protective of me."

"I didn't have *fistfighting* in mind, Dee," Larry said. "A little wrestling, maybe. But definitely nothing violent." He gave a small smile. "Unless you feel threatened by me."

"That'll be the day," I came back. Then I put plan A into action. "What are you going to do for dinner, Larry?" I asked. "Your mom won't be home for hours yet."

"I dunno," he admitted. "I thought I might go down to Pete and Gina's and have a slice of pizza, for old time's sake."

Larry used to drive a delivery wagon for Pete and

Gina when he was in Santa Amelia High. In fact, his car was the wagon. A venerable Volkswagen bug, painted red. I rode with him once or twice. The inside of the car smelled of oregano and garlic.

"Why don't you have dinner with me, then?" I said. "Bruno can whip up something for you. I have a whole pantry full of gourmet groceries that I don't go near."

"Yeah, I noticed that," Larry said. "Fine with me. I'll call Mom from your place, then."

"You got a deal, stranger," I said. I was kidding, but in a way, that's just what we were. Strangers. Larry looked so different, and he acted so mature! I could still picture him getting sick on a single shot of brandy when he came to New York with Harry Grubb last summer. The summer I met Carl Suzuki . . . .

"And Harry left all this to you," Larry said as he finished the last of his New York–cut sirloin. "Who'd have thought it?"

"I certainly never expected it," I said. "He seemed fond of me, but with Harry it was always hard to tell."

"I know what you mean," Larry said. "I knew that Harry liked me when he called me by name. The rest of the time, he pretended he didn't remember." He looked about at the formal dining room. "What do you figure to do with all the money, Dee?" he asked.

"I haven't given it that much thought," I admitted. "But I have lots of time in which to decide. It won't be mine officially for a few years yet. In the meantime, Brian Donnelly, Harry's lawyer, is acting as executor of the will. I get an allowance, plus all reasonable expenses paid."

"What's the allowance?" Larry asked.

When I told him, he gave a long, low whistle. "Some allowance," he said. "You could support a family of four on that."

"I know," I said. "And I honestly feel guilty about it. When I think of all the people in the world who are genuinely in need."

"Now you sound like your mom," Larry said, smiling.

"There are worse things in life I could be than like Linda Fein," I came back quickly.

"Sorry," Larry said. "I didn't mean anything by the remark."

"Well, you don't know what it sounded like to me," I replied somewhat testily. Darnit! What was the matter with me? The first time alone I'd had with Larry Small in I don't know how long, and I was on the verge of an argument.

"Hey, let's not hassle," Larry soothed. "If you're finished with your salad . . ." He broke off and looked at my untouched dinner plate. "Gee, you didn't eat a thing," he said.

"Just not hungry, that's all," I said. "Tell me, what do you feel like doing?"

"I dunno, Dee," Larry said. "Maybe a movie would be neat."

"How about *Fists of Fury*?" I asked. "Or maybe the *Samurai Trilogy*?"

Larry's face lit up. He's crazy about kung fu and Samurai flicks. I had a surprise for him. "That'd be great!" Larry said, "but are you up for driving to L.A.? They never show them here in Santa Amelia."

"We don't have to go to Los Angeles," I said smugly. "All we have to do is walk down the hall to the rec room." I savored the look on Larry's face. "I've got video tapes of them all," I said. "When you wrote to me, I got in touch with a film distributor."

"Now, that's what I call living!" Larry chortled. "Your own film festival. Did you get any Bogie films?"

"Only *Maltese Falcon, Treasure of Sierra Madre, Casablanca,* and *High Sierra,*" I said. "In a few weeks, I'll have *African Queen* and *To Have and Have Not.*"

Larry got up from the table and came around to where I was sitting. He dropped down on one knee and took my hand. "All my life," he said in fruity tones, "I have been wanting to be a kept man. Will you marry me?" He waved his other hand expansively. "Take me away from all that and bring me to all this!"

"But, sir, I hardly know you," I said in a simper, batting my eyes.

"What does it matter?" he said, doing a bad Ronald Colman imitation. "You have all a man could want: Money, muscles, a mustache . . ."

I kissed him lightly on the cheek. "Get up, you goof," I said, "or we miss the movies."

As we walked down the hall, he put his arm around my shoulder. "All we need now is popcorn," he said.

"Not to worry," I replied. "I can have Bruno make some, if you like."

"I was kidding," Larry said. He glanced around him to make sure that Bruno wasn't nearby. "That guy is positively creepy, Dee. I'm surprised he stayed on here after Harry died. Why do you keep him around?"

I shrugged. "He comes with the turf," I said. "In Harry's will, Bruno was asked to stay, and he accepted. But it *is* spooky the way he moves about the house. And you'd think the place was a shrine to Harry's memory! I don't even go into Harry's office. I'm afraid I might disturb something."

"What'd your mom say about you being here alone with him?"

"Not a word. All you have to do is look at Bruno to realize he's asexual," I replied. "But I understand that Helen Grayson will be getting out of Dale Vista soon. She'll be taking over some of Bruno's duties. Harry provided for her hospital bills in his will."

"I heard about that from my mom," Larry said. "That was a close shave you had on Santa Catarina Island this spring."

"Is your mom still trying to marry us off?" I asked. I didn't care to discuss Helen Grayson. The poor woman had enough troubles in her life without rehashing what I still think of as "The Phantom of the Casino" case.

"You know Mom," Larry said. "Her fondest dream is to see me settled down and working at a good, dull, respectable job."

"In Santa Amelia, in a three-bedroom house, with 2.4 children," I added.

"You got it, sport," Larry said. "But since you got so rich, I think she's taken you off the candidate list for Mrs. Larry Small."

"Oh, really?" I said. I don't know why, but the remark nettled me. "Have I grown an extra head? Or has my deodorant failed?"

"Not at all," Larry said. "But now I think she feels you're beyond my station in life."

"What station is that?"

"I'm not sure. I think it's Union Station, in L.A."

I don't know what was wrong, but I couldn't concentrate on the films we saw. We watched *Fists of Fury* and *Casablanca.* A couple of times, I got up and left the room. I didn't go anywhere; I just walked up and down the hall. When I came back, at the end of *Casablanca,* Bogie was just walking off into the foggy night with Claude Rains, saying: "Louie, I think this may be the start of a beautiful friendship. . . ." I didn't even let the cast credits flash on the screen. I snapped on the lights and turned off the video-tape machine.

"What's wrong, Dee?" Larry asked.

"Nothing, nothing at all," I said shortly. "I've just seen the film so many times. It doesn't seem . . . important, somehow."

"Sorry you feel that way, Dee. Do you want me to leave? I'll just call Mom," he said, glancing at his watch. "She should be ready to leave the hospital by now."

"No!" I snapped. "Why should you leave? You just got here!"

Larry got up from the armchair he'd been sitting in and put his arms around me. "Hey, hey," he said. "What's wrong? You're all keyed up."

I disengaged myself abruptly. "Larry Small," I said, "there is absolutely nothing wrong with me. I never felt or looked better in my life. And if you think that I'm about. . . ."

Suddenly, for no reason at all, I felt myself close to tears. I swallowed hard. Larry was standing a few feet away. He'd stepped back when I'd pulled away from his embrace. He had a hurt look on his face.

"Gee, Doris," he said, "I didn't mean anything. Of course you look great. You're beautiful."

"And don't you dare talk in that condescending tone!" I said. "I'm not a child to be humored." What was the matter with me? I had planned this entire evening, weeks ago. Now it was turning sour.

"I think I'd better be going, Dee," Larry said coolly. "You're probably tired. It's been a long day."

"I am not tired!" I insisted. "I feel just great!" I could feel the tears beginning to roll down my cheeks. I saw the look of concern on Larry's face. "You just go home," I said. "I can have Bruno drive you."

"No," Larry said, sitting back down in his chair. "I don't think I will. Doris, there's something wrong. I don't know what it is, but there's something amiss. And I won't leave here until I find out what's really bugging you."

Without knowing why, I suddenly turned and ran toward the door. In a flash, Larry was on his feet, and he grabbed me by the wrist as I was halfway out of the room. I turned and swung an open hand at him.

He moved his head back a fraction of an inch; otherwise I would have caught him full in the face. Then I collapsed in his arms sobbing.

"I don't know what's wrong, Larry," I cried. "I was so looking forward to seeing you. I had Bruno make your favorite dinner. I got the movies you liked. . . . Now it's all rotten!"

Larry held me tight for a few minutes while I cried uncontrollably. Then in a soothing tone, he said, "Come over here, Dee, by the lamp." I obliged. He took my face in one hand. "Look toward the light bulb in the lamp," he requested. I did. "Uh-huh," he said. "Now close your eyes and hold out your hands at arm's length, with your fingers spread apart." I did. "Now open your eyes and look at your hands," he said.

My fingers seemed to have a life of their own! They were trembling visibly. I watched in horror. I've never had the shakes, unless you count the time I had an afterreaction, in New York. But then, the reason was a good one. Someone had been trying to kill me.

Larry guided me to a chair, then brought his chair around opposite mine. We sat inches apart and face to face.

"Remember this game from when we were kids, Dee?" he asked, holding his hands palms upward. I did, of course. I had to put my hands, palms down, a few inches above his. The idea was for Larry to slap one of my hands before I could pull my hand out of the way. I always used to beat him at it, too. It's so easy to tell when he's going to make a move. His eyes give him away. But this time he slapped my hand nine times out of ten. Then he got up and began to walk up and down the room.

"Dee, when did you start losing all the weight?" he asked.

"About six weeks ago."

"And you lost how much in six weeks?"

"That's a rather personal question."

"I'm asking for a personal reason," Larry said. "You are a person very dear to me. Answer me, Dee. It's important."

"I was aiming for thirty pounds," I said, "but I've dropped twenty-six, so far."

"Uh-huh. And who's your doctor?"

"Dr. McDonald."

"What's he been giving you?" Larry asked. "You couldn't have lost that much on a simple diet."

"Ohhh," I exclaimed, "I see what you mean. I thought you meant my regular physician. I haven't lost the weight with Dr. McDonald. I spent two weeks at Aphrodite's." I saw the blank look on Larry's face. "The luxury health spa, down the road," I added, and saw the recognition in his eyes. His expression rapidly changed to another I couldn't identify.

"Isn't that the same one that Leah Lansberg went to?" he asked, naming the lead singer in the group Apollo Twelve. They're a new-wave rock group that's very big just now.

"Could be," I said. "All the biggies go there. My swimming partner was Louise Sorelle."

"Now we're getting somewhere," Larry said. "I'll bet you that Fanny Singer has been there, too."

"How did you know?"

"Never mind," Larry said. "I'll explain in a minute or two. Now tell me this, and think carefully. What kind of medication have you been taking?"

"For the past four weeks, none," I said. "I took the pills they gave me with my meals, but since I left, I haven't taken anything."

"That doesn't make sense. There must be something. Think, Dee."

"The only thing I can think of is my JK-4 shots," I said. "I get two a week since leaving Aphrodite's. But it's only a vitamin concentrate and some kind of extract."

"That's it!" Larry cried. "When did you have your last shot?"

"Three days ago," I replied. "I was due to have another today, but I went to pick you up at the airport. I'd planned to go tomorrow instead."

"Thank God you missed your injection," Larry said. "If you had gone, I might never have known. Or it would have taken me weeks to notice."

"Notice what?" I demanded. "I can't take all this Larry, really I can't. . . . In fact, I feel like I'm going to cry again."

"I'm not surprised," Larry said grimly. "I don't know what your doctor at the spa told you was in those shots. But you're displaying classic symptoms of addiction to amphetamines, Doris!"

7/ *"Hooked?"*

Not wonderful Shirley Redman. Never kind, jovial Dr. Lucius Keene. These people had made me beautiful. They couldn't be the monsters Larry Small was making them out to be.

"You'd better believe it, Dee," Larry said. "I'll bet you've been having trouble sleeping, too."

I admitted it was so, and added, "But only since I've been at home. At Aphrodite's, when I was getting two shots a day, I slept like a top."

"I'll bet you did," Larry said grimly. "They were giving you speed to make you hyperactive and kill your appetite. Then at night, they'd slip you a sleeping pill with your evening meal, so you'd be able to sleep. And I bet that the days when you have your shots at the spa, you have trouble sleeping the same night."

I thought back on the past four weeks. "You're right," I said. "But this is monstrous! And if it *is* going on, I

82

can't believe that Shirley is involved."

"How could she *not* be?" Larry insisted. "Do you think she's some sort of figurehead and Dr. Keene is the evil genius behind it?"

"That's exactly what I think," I replied. "And it could happen. Shirley told me that she engaged Dr. Keene by mail. That he had the best of credentials."

"Where did she check them?"

"She didn't say," I admitted. "But, then again, I didn't ask her."

"Come on, let it go, Dee," Larry said. "She's got to be in it up to her neck."

"What ever became of the idea that a person is innocent until proven guilty?" I demanded. "Besides, I have only your word that I'm showing signs of being an amphetamine user."

Larry sat down again and sighed. "Dee," he said, "where do you think I've been for the past year? In nursery school? I've been covering the pop scene. Don't you read your own paper? Haven't you seen that a congressional committee is trying to look into drug abuse in the pop music and entertainment fields?"

"I also noticed that no one would cooperate with them and testify," I said.

"And a good thing," Larry said. "In my opinion, those legislators were only trying to get themselves publicity and stir up some kind of witch hunt. But their basic claim that the scene is riddled with drug abuse is quite true."

"You have proof?" I asked.

"Only my own eyes and ears," Larry said. "I've seen things backstage at concerts that would have Congress up in arms."

"You mean that everybody's doing drugs?"

"Don't be foolish," Larry said quickly. "There are users and nonusers in all walks of life. For your information, the highest incidence of drug use isn't in the entertainment field at all. It's in medicine—doctors, nurses, and paramedicals."

"Makes sense," I said. "They have the easiest access to drugs."

"And the more unscrupulous ones are like your Dr. Lucius," Larry added. "They become what the musicians call Dr. Feelgoods. They give shots and write prescriptions for anything the show business addicts want."

"All for money?"

"What else?" Larry said, smiling cynically. "You could hardly call them humanitarians." He got up and went over to where the video-tape recorder was hooked up to a wide-screen projection TV. "Tonight's a Monday. Let me see, now." He turned on the TV-set part of the tape setup. The screen flickered, then produced a strong image. It was one of those pop music concert shows. "Yeah, I was right," Larry said. "They show it here on the same night as in San Francisco. Now let's see who's on."

Over the next ninety minutes, Larry pointed out to me those musicians and singers on the show whom he definitely knew to be drug users. I have to say that some were surprises; others weren't.

An absolutely freaky female singer I'd always thought was "on" something was introduced. "Her?" I asked.

"Not a chance," Larry said. "She's very religious and a stone health-food freak. Her idea of getting high is drinking enriched carrot juice."

A few songs later, a comic who had a lily-white image as a youth advocate did his turn. "Now, don't tell me *he* isn't a straight-ahead guy," I said.

"If you don't want to hear it, I won't," Larry said, laughing. "In New York and San Francisco, he's notorious. I tell you, Dee, if I was to ever write another book, I'd give him a full chapter." He turned off the TV set. "That's enough of that guy," Larry said. "He gives me the creeps." He walked over to me and took my hand. "Now do you see what I'm getting at? People aren't always what they seem. In fact, they're hardly *ever* what they seem."

"Well, if you're right about Dr. Keene," I said, "what do I do about it? I mean, am I really an addict now?"

"Depends on your definition. I don't think that in six weeks you'd be so dependent on speed that you couldn't function without it. But see it for what it is, Dee. You missed your twice-a-week shot only a few hours ago. You're irritable, fidgety, you have the shakes."

"Dear Lord above!" I cried. "What can I do?"

"You can see your real doctor, for one," Larry said. "And for another, you're doing the best thing. You didn't get a shot today. Now comes the hard part. You must never go back to Aphrodite's again."

I felt a surge of anger that began at my toenails and slowly ran its way to the roots of my lightened hair. "That's not good enough," I said. "I'm going to put them out of business for what they've done to me. I'll have the law on them. I'll use the paper to publish what they're doing. I'll—"

"Get sued for a million dollars or more," Larry said. "Unless there's residual amphetamine in your bloodstream, you can't prove it. What you're suffering from is a combination of a slight physical addiction and a monster psychological dependence, Dee."

"But a police search of Aphrodite's would turn up all that amphetamine," I insisted.

"What of it?" Larry said. "Some reputable doctors prescribe amphetamines as a short-term aid for dieting patients. It's even used sometimes to calm down hyperactive kids."

"What?"

"That's right. Certain kinds of hyperkinesis in children can be treated with the stuff. It's a fact."

"But little children are given that . . . poison?"

"Dee," Larry said, shaking his head, "any drug, no matter how beneficial, can be abused and become dangerous. What's criminal is not that your Dr. Keene uses speed on his patients. It's the *way* he uses it that's bad."

"So I have to sit here, going through emotional hell, while he gets away with it?"

"And gets rich doing it," Larry said. "Unless, of course, you can nail him for something else that *is* criminal."

"Such as?"

"Geez, I don't know, Dee. All I know about the guy is what you told me. Up until today, I never heard of him."

"Then that's our project for tomorrow," I said firmly. "Can you meet me at the *Register* office in the afternoon?"

"What have you got in mind?"

"I want to have a talk with Jerry Kobrin, the new crime reporter. Dave says that he has a great investigative background. Maybe he can give us something to go on. A way to find out all we can about Dr. Lucius."

"You still feel that your Shirley is blameless?" Larry asked.

"Larry, if you'd met her, talked with her, you'd feel the way I do."

"Okay, Dee," Larry said, "I'm with you. But are you sure that you're up to doing this?"

"Surer than anything. Why?"

"Because unless I'm wrong, you're going to be in rough emotional shape for the next few days. You're going to want to go back there for a shot. Just to feel better. You may have some terribly depressed days for the next few weeks. You've been on an artificial happy trip. Now the roller coaster ride is over."

I called Bruno on the intercom, and he brought the limo around to take Larry home. If Larry was right about his prediction and my condition, I shouldn't have been driving. At the door, Larry stopped me before we went out to where Bruno was waiting in the Mercedes.

"Doris," he said, taking me in his arms, "in all the time I've known you, you've always been . . . well, special to me. We've been kids together. And you've always seemed so . . . in control of yourself. To see you the way you were after dinner . . . it hurt. I just want you to know that whatever it takes to get the crud that did this to you, I'm for it." He grabbed me and gave me a fierce kiss, hugging me so hard I thought my ribs would pop. Then he was out the door.

I turned and walked up the stairs toward my room. I felt tears coming on again. Maybe they were a reaction to the lack of the drug. Maybe it was a relief to know I wouldn't have to fight this alone. I had Larry on my side. I was too outraged and ashamed to tell my parents. My first shot at living apart from my family, and look what had happened. But tomorrow, as Scarlett O'Hara said in *Gone with the Wind,* was another day. And I swore there was going to be a judgment day for Dr. Lucius "Feelgood" Keene!

8/ A Letter from Beyond the Grave

Jerry Kobrin listened to what I had to say, then ordered another cup of black coffee. Larry and I had met him at Sally's Coffeepot, a place near the *Register* building. Jerry's desk is right out in the open in the office, and what we had to say required privacy.

"Well, what do you think, Jerry?" Larry asked.

He ran his fingers through his salt-and-pepper beard. "First thing I'd do is check out Lucius Keene with the state licensing bureau. Make sure he's licensed to practice."

"I saw his license on the wall," I said.

"His license or his diploma?" Jerry asked. "Most doctors hang their diplomas. They're decorative. Licenses aren't."

"Mr. Kobrin," I said, "are you forgetting my own father is a doctor? I know the difference. He had his diploma up there, too."

"Do you recall the medical school?" Larry asked.

"No, darnit," I admitted. "Usually, I look to see if a doctor went to a U.C. medical school because my dad did. I know it wasn't a California school. I would have remembered that."

"And the dates on the license were current?" Jerry asked.

"Yes, they were."

"Back to the drawing board," Larry said glumly. "I guess he's legit. You've seen enough diplomas and licenses, Doris. You know what they look like."

"Okay, that's only *one* tack," Jerry said. "What else can we do?"

"Well, Doris mentioned a few people she'd heard had stayed at Aphrodite's," Larry said. "I know for a fact that some of them are speed freaks. But they had that reputation before they ever went there. If this Keene guy is making addicts of clients, maybe some other guests at the place are acting funny, too."

"Katy Byrd!" I exclaimed.

"Who's that?" Jerry asked.

"She was my next-door neighbor and friend at the spa," I explained. "And she's an incurable gossip. She knows all the dirt that isn't fit to print. She was the one who told me that she saw Fanny Singer there, and Bobbie Blair. . . ."

"She saw Bobbie Blair?" Jerry asked. "How long ago?"

"Last year, she said."

"Exactly *when* last year?" Jerry pressed.

"I don't think she said," I answered. "But she did say that shortly afterward, she got a postcard from Bobbie Blair. From Rio de Janeiro. Then nothing after that."

"Now, that's a real lead," Kobrin said. "No one has seen Blair in over a year. No one in media, that is. It's like she dropped off the face of the earth. Oh, now and then, there's a bit in a column that she's been seen here or there. But no interviews, no pictures. For Blair, that's like a leopard changing her spots. The woman adored having her picture in the paper. And being quoted."

"Maybe she's acting this way because of something that happened at Aphrodite's, then?" I asked.

"It just could be," Kobrin said. "But there's more. I believe that in the last item I read on Blair, she was in South America. But I could swear that was *over* a year ago."

"Aphrodite's is known for its privacy," I said. "She could have come back just for her 'medication.'"

"Then your friend—what's her name?"

"Katy Byrd."

"She may have been one of the last people to see Blair in the past year."

"What of it?" Larry asked.

"If they were all that chummy," Jerry said, "this Byrd lady might know something that would help us. Maybe Blair was acting a bit strange."

"She didn't mention anything to me," I said.

"Why should she?" Jerry came back. "She's known Blair for a while, and you for a couple of weeks. You don't go around airing other people's problems to relative strangers. Not if you're a real friend, you don't."

"You're right!" I said. "I'll get in touch with Katy Byrd."

"And I'll check the morgue on Blair," Jerry said.

"The morgue?" I squeaked. "What do you . . . ?" I trailed off in sudden realization of what Jerry Kobrin meant. The morgue is what we call the back issues of the newspaper. They're all on microfilm in the basement of the *Register* office. "Good idea," I said.

"See what you can come up with on Shirley Redman, too," Larry asked.

"Larry Small," I said, "are you still suspicious of her? I've told you how I feel."

"Okay, okay," he said. "But it wouldn't do any harm. And Jerry, if you will, check out Serena, too. Her other identity."

"Hey, wait a minute, Larry," Kobrin said. "It's one thing to check out Blair. I know where, and generally what dates to check. But Doris says that this Shirley hasn't modeled in years. The morgue doesn't work that way. You have to know what you're looking for."

"Yeah, you're right," Larry said. "It's not like back numbers of the magazine I work for. We're cross-indexed on names."

"You can do that," Kobrin said. "But a newspaper is another thing entirely. Over a thousand items see print in a Sunday edition. We couldn't begin to cross-index individuals less important than, say, international figures. Politicians, popes, stuff like that. People we'd have an obituary already prepared on."

"So much for Serena-slash-line-Shirley Redman," Larry said.

"'Fraid so, laddy," Jerry said. He got to his feet and put a hand in his pocket while picking up the check.

"I'll get it," I said. "You've done me a favor, Jerry."

"What kind of favor?" he said, smiling. "You forget,

if you do find something at that mink-lined fat farm, I've got a great story. Besides, you fed me a swell beef Wellington six weeks ago." He patted his stomach. "And the calories linger on." He took the check and walked toward the cashier's desk.

"Nice guy," Larry said. "Do you think he can take Harry's place?"

"Nobody ever could," I said. "But I like the way his mind works. He didn't tell us we were mistaken. We didn't have to convince him of what we thought. He's got an open mind, and . . . what are you smiling at, Larry Small?"

"Just thinking. If *my* boss talks, I listen. I listen good."

"And you, sir, are flirting with a cup of coffee in your lap," I said. "And that's not amphetamine nerves, either."

Larry drew back in mock terror. Then his face changed. He lowered his voice and asked, "How *do* you feel, Dee?"

"I could barely get up this morning," I said. "And I had a crying fit before lunch. But now that I know what's causing it, I can cope with it. I just get *verry* angry. About what was done to me. Then I snap out of it."

"That's my Doris," Larry said, reaching across the table and patting my hand. Ordinarily, I would have said that I'm no one's Doris but my own. But hearing Larry say it was different somehow.

We got up and left. Larry went to drive his mom to work at the hospital, and I went back to the big house to telephone Katy Byrd.

When I got in, Bruno wasn't in sight. He's usually at

the door when I reach it. Anytime I use the electric gate, it buzzes the house. Not that he would have been there to greet me with an open smile and casual conversation.

I went directly to my room and telephoned Aphrodite's. They answered on the second ring.

"Aphrodite's. Good afternoon."

"Ms. Katy Byrd, please."

"I beg your pardon?"

"Katy Byrd, please. She's a guest there."

"I'm sorry, we don't connect directly to guest rooms. I have no directory of guests. You'll have to speak to Miss Shirley."

"Then I'll speak to her. Put me through, please."

"Who shall I say is calling?"

"Doris Fein. I'm an outpatient."

"Oh, that's different. One moment, please."

In a few seconds, Shirley came on the line.

"Doris, dear! How are you? Dr. Lucius says he missed you yesterday."

I'll bet he did, I thought. But putting a cheery lilt into my voice, I said, "I wanted to talk to Katy. There was something I wanted to tell her."

"Oh, I'm so sorry, Doris," Shirley said. "You can't talk to her. She left the spa. Her stay was over."

"Did she say where she was going?" I asked. "I mean, did she go home to San Francisco?"

"I didn't ask her, dear. But I imagine so."

"Thanks so much, Shirley," I said. "I'll try her there."

"And Doris?"

"Yes?"

"Will you be coming in for your JK-4? Dr. Lucius seemed concerned."

I hesitated before answering. Was Shirley really a part of this, as Larry suspected? I got an idea. "I'm sorry, truly sorry," I said, "but that special person is in town. Remember the one we spoke of?"

"Oh, that's it!" she said, and I heard her warm laugh over the wires. "Well, that's much more important, isn't it? Have a good time, Doris, dear. But do watch your diet, won't you?"

"I will, Shirley."

"Remember. Beautiful inside and out, dear," she said. "Come by when you find time."

I put the phone down with relief. If Shirley were part of it, she would have been pressing me to get over to the spa—before the symptoms showed up badly. From her tone of voice, she only wished me well. No pressure at all to come in. No, it had to be Lucius Keene's own little plot. I thumbed through my address book and came up with Katy Byrd's number in San Francisco.

The phone rang a few times; then a cool woman's voice came on the line. "Byrd residence."

"Katy Byrd, please," I said.

"I'm sorry," said the voice, "Mrs. Byrd is not in town."

"Do you have a referral number?" I asked. "I'm a personal friend of Ms. Byrd's."

"What is your name?" asked the voice.

"What is *your* name, and who are you?" I countered.

"This is Mrs. Byrd's secretary, Miss Ellenstein," said the voice.

"Well, I'm Doris Fein. I met Katy at Aphrodite's in Santa Amelia. She gave me this number."

"Miss Fein, so far as I know, Mrs. Byrd is still at Aphrodite's," said Miss Ellenstein. "Have you tried there?"

"Yes, I did. They told me she had left."

There was a silence at the other end for a full thirty seconds. I was about to check to see if Miss Ellenstein was still on the line, when she spoke. "This is very strange. I usually know each and every stop on Mrs. Byrd's itinerary. She was to have been in Santa Amelia for six weeks, then return home."

"Ah, that's it," I said. "She's probably between points. She isn't at the spa, but she hasn't gotten home yet. I'll call tomorrow."

"Very well, Miss Fein?"

"That's *Ms.* Fein. Doris Fein."

"Very well, Ms. Fein, I'll leave a message that you called. Your number please?"

I gave Miss Ellenstein my home number by mistake, then quickly corrected it to Harry's. After you've had one telephone number for almost all your life, it's hard to change. I hung up, puzzled. Shirley had said Katy Byrd had left Aphrodite's. But she didn't say exactly when. From my conversations with Katy, I knew that she didn't drive; she'd flown in from San Francisco. The flights for San Francisco leave John Wayne Airport almost on the hour. I spent the next hour or so on the phone with regularly scheduled airlines that serve the Bay area from John Wayne Airport. No Katy Byrd listed on any of their flights.

I got out my Yellow Pages and checked charter flights. No soap. I was beginning to smell a large rat. About the size of a man named Lucius Keene. Maybe.

Then it happened—for the first time in six weeks. I heard a rumbling sound that could have come from only one source. Petunia. She was back!

I called Bruno on the intercom and got no answer. Very strange for him. I debated whether or not to give in to the demands of my inner porcine friend. But I'd worked so hard to shed the excess poundage that I struggled bravely. Deciding on perhaps a light salad, I walked down the hall and this time took the main stair-case down to the main floor. As I headed for the dining room, I noticed that the door to Harry's office was ajar.

"Bruno?" I called. No answer. I walked into Harry's office to find Bruno standing behind Harry's big old desk. Not doing anything, not stirring. Just standing there.

"Bruno, didn't you hear me?" I asked.

"No, Ms. Fein."

"What were you doing in here?"

"Straightening up," he replied.

"Well, if you're done," I said, "I'd like a bite to eat. A salad, I think."

"Caesar okay?" he asked.

Shrimp Louie . . . Shrimp Louie, Petunia insisted.

"A Caesar will be fine," I said firmly and virtuously. I heard Petunia's reply, but it wasn't printable.

Bruno went noiselessly out the office door, and I wandered aimlessly about the room I seldom entered. I inspected the Remingtons and other American artists' work that Harry had loved so. I even sat down at the big, old-fashioned swivel chair behind Harry's desk. It was a bit incongruous to note a rather modern-looking push button at the back of one of the desk's cubbyholes. I'd never noticed it before. I debated with myself for a second before I pushed it.

I wasn't sure what would happen. Harry had a number of alarm devices planted in the house. I couldn't be sure if this was one of them. For all I knew, sirens would wail and bells go off. I sighed inwardly when no racket greeted me. In fact, nothing happened at all. Bruno didn't materialize, so the button wasn't a paging system. Maybe a silent alarm? I swiveled around in the chair, and nearly fell off in surprise.

The entire wall section behind Harry's desk had slid to one side. There, staring me in the face, was an alarming array of electronic panels, a keyboard that looked like a typewriter's but somehow wasn't, a darkened TV screen, and a big, modern electric typewriter with a lot of electrical leads going into it. I had to laugh aloud. No wonder Harry Grubb prided himself on his inside information. I'd often wondered myself where all his dirt on the greats came from. I was looking at an up-to-date word processor, coupled to an elaborate minicomputer!

I recognize a word processor when I see one. I should. The medical group my father belongs to has one. They're great labor-saving devices. Especially if you do periodic billing, as doctors do. They can store and retrieve routine correspondence, send out letters that are all original copies . . . well, depending on the degree of sophistication of the machine, a word processor linked to a computer can do an amazing variety of things. I had used the one at my dad's office as part of my duties as his secretary and receptionist.

I found that the keyboard was in exactly the right position for a man Harry's height, if he swiveled 180 degrees in his desk chair. I had to make an adjustment in height and reach. I put out my hand for the power switch and, in doing so, touched the console. It was warm to the touch. Someone had been running the machine.

Try as I might, I couldn't envision Bruno running this complex setup. But then again, who'd have thought Bruno could be a cordon bleu chef either? I turned on the machine. The lights glowed and the green-on-green TV screen lit up. But nothing flashed on it. I checked the disk holders.

A word processor records information on little floppy disks, the size of a 45 rpm record. You put the disk into a slot and it can play back what's on the disk on the TV screen, or it can print it out on paper, through the typewriter part. It's somewhat spooky to see the typewriter print out. It doesn't take but seconds to type what the fastest secretary would take minutes to do.

I got up and inspected the shelves above the word processor. I found what I was looking for right away. The disks for the machine are stored in loose-leaf albums. Each disk can store the equivalent of 350 printed pages. They fit into sleeves in the ring binders, and each page they occupy has room for a title or summary of what's on the disk. I looked at the binders, neatly arranged on the shelves. The titles were meaningless to me. They were marked in some shorthand system known only to Harry. I took a binder down from the shelf and leafed through it. The entries identifying the contents of the disks were as cryptic as the titles on the spines of the binders.

I was about ready to give up. With good reason. These machines can store immense quantities of information, but if you don't know the coding system by which they're entered, they could just as easily be hieroglyphics from ancient Egypt. Then I saw a well-thumbed manual for the word processor itself. Evidently, Harry hadn't had the machine for long. He had been referring to the operator's manual a great deal. I swung the chair around, placed the manual on the desk, and sat down to read.

"What are you doing?" Bruno said from the doorway. It was the first time I'd ever heard Bruno raise his voice. Indignation was in every word. I'd sullied some holy of holies: Harry's private office.

"Trying to figure out how this machine works, Bruno," I replied in a matter-of-fact tone. "Harry seems to have invented his own encoding system."

"You know how it works?" Bruno said as he set down my salad. Evidently, he'd wondered where I was when he came into the study with my meal. He'd kept the salad in his hand as he searched for me.

"I know how this model works, basically," I said. "The computer tie-in is different from anything I've seen, though. And Harry's system is . . . well, I don't know what it is."

"Move, please," Bruno said, coming around the desk.

I obliged, and he sat down at the console, after twirling the chair around. He took a disk from a small drawer of the table the machine sat upon. He inserted it into the disk player, punched a few keys on the console, and the green TV screen came alive. He got up from the chair and gestured to me to sit down. I did, and he reached over my shoulder and indicated a key.

"Punch this to get the next line," he said.

"Bruno!" I exclaimed. "You can run this thing? You know the code system?"

"It's on the screen, Ms. Fein," he said. "Will you have your dinner in here?"

"Yes, yes," I said abstractedly. "You can bring in my plate and silver." I wasn't even interested in the food anymore. I was in shock. Not that Bruno could run the complicated computer and word processor. It was what was unfolding before my eyes.

Dear Doris, the green-on-green type on the screen read, *Being the incurable snoop you are, it was just a matter of time before you found my little secret filing system. Congratulations!*

It was a letter to me from Harry Grubb. From beyond the grave!

9/ Bingo!

A half hour later, my salad still untouched, I read the last words that flashed upon the screen. I sat in silent admiration of the mind of the late Harry Grubb. He'd anticipated that I'd find his little secret filing system. He explained his entry codes and where I could find further information on each entry.

What I had in my possession was one of the most remarkable crime libraries in the world. For the past six years, Harry had been systematically entering every criminal event of note into the memory of this machine. He'd broken all the transgressions down into categories. For instance, there were three disks on unsolved murders, with a cross-index to sex of victim, age of same, geographic location, and current status of the investigation. These entries were in a shorthand system of Harry's own devising. Each entry was accompanied by an index number, referring to a specific edition of

The Register and the news wire service that was the source of the item.

If I had, say, an unsolved murder, I could get the name and a brief summary of the deed. Then I could get additional details from the microfilmed morgue at *The Register*. The ring binders contained a veritable cornucopia of criminality, from murder to embezzlement, from armed robbery to kidnapping. You name it; Harry had it all down. I punched a button on the console and, in wonder, reread the last words of Harry's letter to me.

I hope that you will continue to make entries in my unsolved crimes file, Doris. It doesn't take long, at the end of each day. As I am not a touch typist, I have found Bruno invaluable. He knows the codes and can make this machine fly. I sit down with the evening edition of The Register *and dictate to Bruno such items as I want entered into the machine's memory. I have so far entered over five years of assorted mayhem and misappropriation of money into the memory banks. Some entries that have longer histories are indexed.*

Now that you have snooped out my secret, I draw your attention to Alois Biegler, or Bruno, as he prefers to be called. He can be of great use to you. When I first sprang him from a hospital for the criminally insane in Illinois, he'd already attracted the attention of a few doctors. He has a rare mental condition, which has prompted some psychologists and psychiatrists to write him up.

Despite my expending a great deal of money in treat-

ing his condition, he's not much improved. The condition isn't quite as bad as autism. But Bruno seems incapable of acting or giving any information unless he's specifically asked for it. That's why, when an intruder killed both his mother and father years ago, and Bruno was found with a bloodied knife at the scene, he ended up in jail, then in an institution. No one knew how to ask him what had happened. They assumed he was substandard in intelligence. He is far from it. But it's all locked up inside his head. Like the machine you are reading this letter on, Bruno is a wellspring of useful information and skills. But you must know how to ask, to make those skills and data available. To date, I seem to be the one person he responds to. I have left him specific instructions on this machine, which he operates with consummate skill. If you have not discovered the machine and this letter after one year's time, he has instructions to destroy the disk and shut down the Grubb unsolved-felony file. The best of luck to you, Doris Fein. And heed my advice. Marry that Japanese lawyer of yours. There, I've had the last word, after all. Harry Grubb.

A strange feeling came over me on reading Harry's words. You'd think that reading such a message would make one feel that Harry wasn't dead after all. But it had the opposite effect on me—a finality I hadn't felt even at the reading of Harry's will. It was as though in imparting his secret files to me, posthumously, Harry had personally handed over the keys to the house.

While I was thinking about it, Bruno came in to pick up my plate.

"Bruno," I said, "I've cracked the code on Harry's files."

"Yes, Ms. Fein," Bruno said. And it didn't bother me. Now that I understood how Bruno's mind worked, his laconic replies made sense. He wasn't rejecting me or acting as though I didn't belong in Harry's house. In his literal-mindedness, Bruno was simply obeying Harry's last orders. And evidently had still been doing so through the messages left for him on the word processor and computer.

"You and Mr. Grubb were very close, weren't you, Bruno?" I asked.

"Yes, Ms. Fein."

"You two were all alone in this house, but kept each other company."

"Yes, Ms. Fein."

"How did you keep each other company, Bruno?"

"We talked, Ms. Fein." That kind of shook me up. A conversation with Bruno would have to be awfully one-sided.

"You talked with Mr. Grubb?"

"He talked," Bruno said. "I listened."

"And what were you doing with the word processor when I came in, Bruno?" I asked. I already knew, from Harry's letter. But I wanted to see how Bruno would handle being called upon for a response that wasn't a simple yes or no.

"I was entering the crime news from today's *Register*, Ms. Fein."

"How did you know which ones to enter and which ones to leave out?" I pressed on. Now, this question had to elicit more than one sentence in reply.

But I was wrong. Bruno went to a ring binder on one of the shelves above the machine and took it down. He opened up the book and withdrew a single disk, which he inserted in the processor. He keyed in an action, and on the screen flashed the words *Master File, Alphabetical.* Below this title, in order, was a series of names, each with its accompanying code entry.

"How does it work, Bruno?" I asked.

"If I see a name in the paper in the crime news, I check against the master file. If it's on the file, I enter it on the proper disk," Bruno said. "The code number alongside the name is for the disk and volume it belongs in. The disk entry will also have the cross-index to *The Register*'s microfilm morgue. Anything legal is cross-indexed to the data bank."

"Data bank? You mean the machine's memory?"

"No, the data bank. There are seven of them. You telephone the data bank for any lawsuit, prosecution for a crime, decisions of the various supreme courts, appellate divisions. In Illinois, there's a huge computer that has all that stored. You link to your computer by telephone. You ask the data bank what you want to know. It flashes all the information on the screen. If you want a permanent record of it, you record it on the processor's memory. If you want it in print, you push the *print* button, and the printer over there types it out."

I stared goggle-eyed at Bruno. It was the longest I've ever heard him talk. I must admit that with his toneless inflection and deadpan expression, there was more warmth in the late Harry Grubb's letter to me than in Bruno's delivery. But boy, did he talk!

"Bruno, you are an amazing person," I said.

"Yes, Ms. Fein," he replied. I wouldn't swear to it, but I think I saw a certain self-satisfaction on the man's face. Then again, as my dad has pointed out to me many times, we tend to see what we want to see. But I knew I would never again be intimidated by Bruno's presence or his silent way of moving about the house. You only fear what you don't understand. I made up my mind that it would be a waste not to utilize Bruno's special knowledge, as Harry had done. However, it seemed so cold, using Bruno as though he were some sort of automaton . . . a robot.

"Bruno?" I asked.

"Yes, Ms. Fein?"

"Did you enjoy working with Harry Grubb on the crime file?"

"Yes, Ms. Fein."

"Are you proud of your training and accomplishments? I mean, you can drive, you're a French chef, you fix things around the house, and now I discover you're a computer genius. Does this make you feel proud of what you've done?"

"Yes, Ms. Fein," Bruno said, "it does." And so help me, Bruno smiled! Not much of a smile. More like the corners of his mouth twitching upward for a split second. I felt honored and privileged to see that almost-smile. And it laid to rest my qualms about utilizing Bruno's expertise. He *could* be reached, emotionally!

"Well, Bruno," I said, "we are going to continue with

the file. Just as Harry Grubb did. I must confess that I'm a novice at machines like this. I'm just learning at college. Do you think you can help me master it?"

"Yes, Ms. Fein," he said flatly. Then I realized what I had said. Perhaps Bruno thought I wanted to dispense with his services.

"Well, I see no point in it," I said. "You're miles ahead of me. I could never catch up. We'll do it the way you and Harry did it. I'll read the papers and pick the items; you'll enter them."

"*Yes,* Ms. Fein," he said. And this time, there was no mistake. He *did* smile. I returned my attention to the screen of the processor. Not that I was about to start checking names. I wanted to look away from Bruno's face for a second. That small smile represented a major reaching out for him. And it expressed trust in me. I was frankly a bit embarrassed.

Then my eye lit on something. An entry on the alphabetical index. *Blair, Lucinda,* it read. Followed by a series of coded symbols.

In a rush, all the events of the past six weeks came crowding in. It reminded me of Bobbie Blair and Aphrodite's. But who was *Lucinda* Blair? I asked Bruno the meaning of the symbols that followed the entry under the name. For a reply, he came over and examined the digits. Then he went to the shelves and took down another binder. He handed it to me. The volume had a title: *Murder?*

Bruno put the disk into the machine and punched a few keys, and the screen divulged this information:

BLAIR, LUCINDA. Heiress to Magnus Industries for-

*tune. Death by drowning off Costa del Sol, Spain. Fell
off yacht while drunk. Also present her only relative,
Roberta. Family physician signed death certificate.
Possible collusion? Over 75 million bucks at stake.* This
capsule summary was followed by the code I'd already
figured out. It was the fuller story, with follow-ups and
where I'd find it in the *Register* morgue.

I stood up, after punching the *print* button. I tore off
the entry from the roller of the typewriter/printer part
of the machine. "Bruno, I have to go downtown. I need
to go through the *Register*'s morgue to check out this
entry." I handed him the tear sheet. "Where do I find
it?"

"That's for six years ago," Bruno said. "Too bad. We
have two years of *The Register* here, on microfilm. Mr.
Grubb died before we had it all transferred to his files.
The code is for May of 1975."

"Thank you, Bruno," I said. "I'm headed for the *Register* office. Would you please call Larry Small at home
and ask him to meet me there?"

"Yes, Ms. Fein."

It was lucky that I wasn't spotted by the Santa Amelia
police as I drove downtown. I'm sure I exceeded the
limit. Not by much, but I was hurrying. I pulled into the
parking lot the same time as Larry did in his mother's
car. Larry lives only ten minutes from the *Register*
office.

"That was fast," he said as I got out of the Gumdrop
and strode toward him. "What's going on? Some emergency?"

"You could say so," I replied. "It's more like a hurry-up hunch I have to check out. Come on, we're going to the morgue."

"Aha! You got something on Lucius Keene?"

"No, on Bobbie Blair."

"What's she got to do with it?"

"Maybe nothing. Maybe a lot," I said mysteriously. I just didn't want to admit that I hadn't the flimsiest pattern of logic to justify the search of the archives. Just a nagging feeling in the back of my mind. There had to be a connection. Otherwise, why had Shirley reacted so strangely the day I mentioned Blair's name?

The staff room was nearly empty. The morning edition had been put to bed, and the night-edition staff wasn't all there yet. It may sound strange, but the folks who work on the morning edition work at night and in the afternoon, while the people who put together the evening paper work in the early morning.

There's someone at the paper twenty-four hours a day, though. But at certain hours there's only a skeleton crew. One of the people who's always there is the switchboard operator. I was about to walk by, on my way downstairs to the microfilm storage, when she called out to me.

"Miss Fein?" I stopped. "You are Miss Fein, aren't you?" she asked. She was a lady in her sixties, wearing a blue print dress and blue hair to match.

"Yes, I'm Ms. Fein," I said.

"I thought so," she said. "I haven't seen you since you were little. You're Dr. Michael Fein's daughter, aren't you?"

"Yes."

"I thought so! Your father treated me for cataracts ten years ago. I owe him my eyesight."

"Nice to know you . . . er . . . ?"

"Sally. Sally Sherman," she said. Then she smiled a lovely warm smile and put her hand to her forehead. "I must be getting old. I didn't call you over to pass the time of day . . . or night. I have some mail for you."

"Here?" I asked. "I never get mail here. Anything that comes in . . ."

"We forward to your home," Sally Sherman concluded. "But this came in after we sent off the regular package to your home." She handed me a picture postcard. It was a shot of the harbor of Rio de Janeiro, complete with Sugar Loaf Mountain in the background. I turned it over and my stomach formed into a hard, cold knot.

Dear Doris, it read. *Lost your home address, so am writing care of* The Register. *Rio is wonderful! May stay here for some time. Watch your diet. Will write again soon. Love, Katy Byrd.*

"What's wrong, Dee?" Larry asked. "Bad news?"

"Strange news," I said. Then I explained how I'd tried to get hold of Katy Byrd in San Francisco and what her secretary had told me.

"Easily checked," Larry said. "Do you have the number with you? We can call San Francisco and see what her secretary knows about this." He took the card from my hand and examined it. "Neatly typed," he said. I grabbed the card and reexamined it.

"You're right," I said. "Nice even pressure on the

letters. A professional job. There's only one thing wrong."

"What?"

"Katy Byrd can't type a lick. She told me so herself. That's why she has a secretary. As to the signature, who knows? I've never had a letter from her, so anyone could have signed Katy's name to this."

"Let's get her secretary on the phone," Larry said.

Naturally, I'd left the number in my address book, at home in my room. We had to call Bruno first, and once we got the unlisted number, I dialed Katy Byrd's residence from Dave Rose's office. Dave had finally gone home for the night. After a half-dozen rings, Miss Ellenstein came on the line. I quickly identified myself and told her of the postcard I'd received.

"It's fortunate that you reached me tonight, Ms. Fein," said Miss Ellenstein. "I would have been gone by tomorrow. I got a postcard, too."

"Are you joining her in Rio?" I asked.

"Hardly," she replied coolly. "The card said I was let go. I am to draw six months' salary. The house here in San Francisco is to be sold. Kat . . . Mrs. Byrd is staying in Brazil. I don't understand it, either. In the past, I've always traveled with her. When she was married to Mr. Byrd, we went all over the world together."

"Miss Ellenstein," I said, "I'm going to level with you. I think that Katy is in trouble. I don't believe she's in Rio."

"The postmark was legible. It was from Rio, all right."

"But what about the handwriting?"

"It was typed. That's what . . . hurt so. She's hired a new secretary. Ms. Fein, I've been with Katy Byrd for eight years. Now this, with no explanation. . . ."

"What about her signature?" I asked. "Is it really hers?"

"Without a doubt," Miss Ellenstein said. "I've seen it often enough. In fact, *signed* it often enough."

"You signed her correspondence?"

"Only routine matters. Personal correspondence and checks, she alone signed."

"Is it a difficult signature to duplicate?" I asked.

"No, it's quite childish, actually. In fact, she . . . oh, my goodness! Do you think something has happened to her?"

"I don't know," I admitted. "And I don't want to alarm you unduly. However, it doesn't sound like Katy, letting you go without any notice. And without telephoning, at least."

"That's why I was so hurt," Miss Ellenstein said. "She was always the most considerate person. . . . Oh, my! Listen to me. I'm talking as though . . ."

"I know what you were about to say," I interjected, "and don't. All we have is a hunch and a feeling that something's not right. I may know more tomorrow. I'll keep in touch with you, Miss Ellenstein." I hung up, and Larry and I went downstairs to begin searching the microfilm back issues of *The Register.*

"Got it!" I cried. "Here's the Blair story."

"Bobbie Blair?" Larry asked.

"No, her aunt. Lucinda Blair." I read the story in its

entirety. Lucinda Blair and her niece, Roberta, were cruising in the family yacht through the Mediterranean. There was a party on board, with some of the local Spanish dignitaries and some expatriate Americans. Lucinda Blair was known for her parties, her beauty, and her many men friends. She'd been married five times; some of the husbands had been movie stars. One of them had been an Italian count. She was in her late fifties, but still one of the reigning beauties of the world. It was rumored that she'd had numerous face lifts, and all sorts of health cultists and quacks flocked to her.

It's a familiar story. Rich as she was, Lucinda Blair couldn't stop the clock. When she realized she was getting on, she expended huge amounts of money trying to find the Fountain of Youth through hormones, special diets, and plastic surgery.

While the party on her yacht was in full swing, Lucinda disappeared. Nobody thought much of it. They assumed she had gone belowdecks with her latest boyfriend, a Spaniard she had met that week. By the end of the night, when she didn't show, no one thought to look in her cabin. That would have been indiscreet.

It wasn't until noon the following day that it was discovered she wasn't in her cabin. Then the search began. A day later, her body was washed up on the shore, some few miles from where the yacht had been anchored.

A medical report, filed by the family physician, was confirmed by the Spanish authorities. She had somehow struck her head while at the party and, unnoticed, had fallen over the side of the yacht and been drowned. I read the section on the report, and a name leaped out at me. Then I checked an inside page, spooling the microfilm ahead. There was a picture of her and her guests on the yacht, taken the very day she had the party. It didn't do me much good to look at it. The microfilm isn't printed black on white. It's white on black, like a negative, so I couldn't make out the people in the picture. But I could certainly read the caption below the photograph. It was of two men and two women. The caption read:

Pictured just hours before the tragedy are (left to right): Mrs. Lucinda Blair, her escort, Mario Arruza, niece Roberta Blair, and family physician Dr. Lucius Keene.

"Larry," I said.

"Yeah, Dee?"

"Bingo!" I replied.

10/ Killer Keene?

"You've done an incredible research job here," Jerry Kobrin said to me. "I knew about the Blair case, of course. But over the past six years, Bobbie's antics in the papers have overshadowed the circumstances surrounding her aunt's death. You hardly see it mentioned in print anymore. Case closed."

"What else do you know about it?" I asked. "I've read all the accounts that ran in *The Register.*"

"Then you know as much as almost anyone," Jerry said. "We got it all off the international news wire services. I don't know if there was TV coverage. Depends on what else happened that week. All the news doesn't get televised, you know."

"And all the news doesn't get into the papers, either," Larry added. "I should know."

"Yeah, I read your novel," Jerry said to Larry. "A nice job."

"Thanks for the kind words, Jerry," Larry said. "But it was the last assignment I had that was worth the

116

game. I've been covering routine interviews and record-store openings ever since."

"You're unhappy with the job?" I asked. "This is the
first I've heard of it, Larry."

"Face it, we haven't talked too much," Larry said.
"The first day I was in town, you were so wired by the
stuff Dr. Keene was pumping into you, we never got
around to talking. Since we found out what's going on
at Aphrodite's. . . ."

"What may be going on," Jerry corrected.

". . . *May* be going on at Aphrodite's," Larry continued, "we haven't spoken of anything but Dr. Keene
and the spa."

"About that," Jerry said, "I'd be interested in how
you expect to get the goods on Dr. Keene. All you really
have is circumstantial evidence. Yes, he was on the
yacht. But he's an expert in geriatrics, the science of
aging. He's a plastic surgeon as well. That's exactly the
sort of family physician Lucinda Blair would have with
her. Where's his motive? If he was part of Lucinda
Blair's death, the retainer fees he got from her would
stop. He'd be killing the goose that laid the golden
egg."

"Unless he was mentioned in her will," I said
brightly. "And I know how to find out, too!"

"Really? How?" Jerry asked.

"Professional ethics," I said, winking. "I have to pro-
tect my source." I went to the pay phone on the wall
at Sally's Coffeepot and dialed Bruno at home. He answered on the first ring. I told him what I needed to
know.

"Right away, Ms. Fein," he said. "I'll call the data

bank in Illinois on the other line if you want to hold."

I glanced back to where Jerry Kobrin and Larry Small were seated in a booth. "No, I don't think so, Bruno," I said. "Let me give you the phone number here. Call me back once you know. I'll be here for another half hour, at least."

"Okay, Ms. Fein," Bruno said, and hung up. I went back to the booth.

"What's the word, pretty bird?" Larry asked.

"I'll know in a few minutes," I said. "I'll be getting a call."

"Shouldn't you tell Sally?" Jerry asked.

"She knows me," I replied. "One of the advantages of being a native. At one time, everyone in Santa Amelia knew each other. But since the big exodus from the East to California, you're lucky to know your neighbors lately."

Jerry Kobrin waved at our waitress and ordered another cup of coffee. When it arrived, he emptied a package of Sweet 'n Low into it. He saw my glance. "Maybe I'm kidding myself. I eat a big meal, then top it off with coffee and artificial sweetener. I'm reconciled to my weight. But I have to say," he continued, "I don't see why you're so ticked off at Aphrodite's. They did some job on you. When you came to the office last week, I couldn't believe it was the same Doris Fein I'd had dinner with six weeks before."

"But at what cost?" I said. "Not the money; I have that. Can't you see that administering drugs the way he does, it's just a matter of time before that man Keene kills someone? And I think he may already have done that. Six years ago. And now Katy Byrd is missing."

"You don't know that, either," Larry said. "You did get a postcard from her."

"If it was really from her. You know what her secretary said."

"The word of a disgruntled, recently fired employee?" Jerry asked, raising his eyebrows. "Hardly a reliable source."

"I can tell when people are telling the truth," I insisted. "I heard that woman's voice on the phone. She was concerned about Katy, too." Just then the pay phone rang. Sally picked it up at the cash register and waved me over. I spoke quickly with Bruno, and didn't care for what I heard. I went back to the booth with a long face.

"Something wrong?" Larry asked.

"You could say so," I said. "Jerry was right. Lucius Keene wasn't mentioned in Lucinda Blair's will. It all went to several organized and reputable charities, with the bulk of it to Bobbie Blair. As of the day Lucinda Blair drowned, Dr. Lucius was out of a job."

"There goes your scenario, Dee," Larry said. "And it would be natural for Keene to open a health clinic and spa with Shirley Redman. He had all the background, and with Blair, he had the society connections to make it possible. After all, he was personal youth and beauty doctor to one of the great beauties of the society world."

"So I just sit back and let him get away with drugging people, not telling them what he's doing? I feel like I've been swindled."

"Swindled how?" Jerry asked. "You lost the weight, like they promised you. You aren't addicted . . ."

"No thanks to them," I put in. "Larry made me aware of it."

"For all you know, Lucius Keene was tapering you off the drug," Jerry insisted. "You'd already dropped from two shots a day to two per week."

"But I didn't know what was in the shots," I said doggedly.

"You don't know the ingredients in half the prescriptions any doctor writes," Jerry countered.

"Maybe *you* don't," I came back, "but my dad's a doctor. I read prescriptions."

"Then you know how hard it is to convict a doctor of wrongdoing," Jerry said. "Look at the Coppolino case in Florida. Murder was done, and how many trials did it take to get the truth?"

"That's it!" I cried. "The Coppolino case!"

"I don't follow," Larry said. "Who are you guys talking about?"

I didn't want to tip my hand. But I knew about the Coppolino case. I'd read a whole book about it. Coppolino was an anesthesiologist. He'd used a muscle relaxant, succinylcholine chloride, to simulate heart failure. It was thought that he had done away with three people: his father-in-law, his girlfriend's husband, and his own wife. He was convicted only of his wife's murder.

I explained the circumstances to Larry, who kept shaking his head. "The motive, Dee, the motive," he persisted. "You've determined that Keene wasn't in Lucinda Blair's will."

"Ah, but Bobbie Blair was," I said. "In the Coppolino case, it was the girlfriend who actually administered the drug to her own husband. She got it from Coppolino."

"So you think Bobbie Blair and Keene were in cahoots?" Jerry asked.

"Could be."

"Also might not be," Larry said.

"In any event, Shirley must be told the sort of man she's in business with," I said. "And then, there's the disappearance of Katy Byrd."

"All the way to Brazil," Larry said, "and you got a card from her. If I were Shirley and you told me all this, I'd think you were on something. And not anything you got from Dr. Keene, either."

"Well, I intend to warn her," I said. "She's told me that she hired Keene by mail. She may not even know about the Lucinda Blair affair."

"If she didn't read the newspapers," Jerry said, "which I doubt. If you're so convinced Keene is shady, what makes you so sure that Shirley isn't part of it?"

"All you have to do is meet her," I replied. "She's good, she's honest . . ."

"A Girl Scout leader, too?" Larry cracked.

"I don't think that's funny, Larry," I said sharply. "And I'm not giving up on this thing, either."

"Sorry, Dee," Larry said, then looked sharply at me. "Are you okay? I mean the . . ."

"Drugs?" I asked. "I think so. I haven't had a crying fit for days, now."

"Well, I find all this far from conclusive," Jerry said,

getting up. "And there's still a paper to get out. I have to get back to the office. And if I don't see you, Ms. Fein, Happy Hanukkah."

"You too," I said as Jerry left. Larry and I went to the desk, and despite my protests, Larry paid for the coffees. We went out onto the street, which was aglow with Christmas decorations. Several downtown stores had Christmas music piped out into the street.

The general ambience of the downtown area may have been one of holiday cheer, but I was feeling rather low. My carefully constructed theory had been logically shot down by both Larry and Jerry Kobrin. But I'd be darned if I could bring myself to give up. A thought crossed my mind and I had to laugh aloud.

"What's the joke, Dee?" Larry asked.

"I just realized that I may have been living in Harry Grubb's house too long. I'm acting the same way Harry did when he had a hunch or smelled a rat."

"Could be," Larry admitted. "But then again, Harry was right a lot of the time with his hunches." He smiled. "Bruno's innocence was one of Harry's hunches."

Larry's remark triggered an idea. I suddenly grabbed him and gave him a big kiss. "Larry, you're a genius!" I cried. "Thanks a million for the idea!"

"What idea?" Larry said, confused.

"I'll tell you later," I said. "Can you get home okay?"

"Sure."

"I'll call you if my hunch pays off," I said. "I have to get back to the house."

"What for?"

"I have to speak with Bruno."

"Good luck," Larry said. "A conversation with Bruno is like a chat with a statue." He waved to me as I jogged toward the *Register* parking lot and got into the Gumdrop. So Jerry and Larry wanted hard evidence, did they? If my theory was right, I knew how to prove it!

Three hours later, I had it. It had taken calls into two data banks, and easily thirty cross-references in Harry's unsolved file, but I had pieced together what I needed to know.

"That's it, Bruno," I said. "I know how Keene could have done it, and I have the motive now. But I must warn Shirley of the monster she has under her roof."

The telephone rang, and Bruno answered. He spoke a few words and handed the phone to me. "It's John Perry, Ms. Fein," he said. "The photographer at *The Register.*"

I grabbed at the phone. This could be the final link! "Hello, John?" I asked. "Did the picture come up well?"

"Sharp and clear," he said. "I also went through the files of photos. There were some other pictures that came over the wire service. We only used the one we ran. I've made copies, and you'll have them tomorrow, with your regular mail from *The Register.* But no doubt that the guy in the picture is your Dr. Keene. I've seen him in town."

"John, when budget hearings come up, you may be in for a raise," I said happily. "You can for sure count on a Christmas bonus."

"Just doing my job, Ms. Fein."

"You mean you won't take the bonus?" I asked.

"I didn't say *that*," Perry said, laughing.

I hung up and quickly dialed Aphrodite's. The phone rang for a while, then Shirley herself picked up the receiver. I recognized her voice.

"Shirley, this is Doris Fein," I said. "I must meet with you."

"Of course, Doris, dear," she said. "How about tomorrow evening, say, sixish?"

"It can't wait," I persisted. "I'm just up the road. Can't I come over?"

"I'm ready for bed, dear," Shirley replied. "And there isn't a member of the staff here. We don't accept guests during the week before Christmas, and no one is scheduled in until after the first of the year."

"I didn't want to use the facilities," I explained. "I've come across some information you should know. It's about Dr. Lucius."

"What about Lucius?"

"He's not what he seems to be. There are things in his past."

"I can't imagine what you mean, Doris. His ratings are extremely high. I checked him with several sources, professional sources, before I hired him."

"Your sources were all as to his medical standing?"

"Naturally."

"Well, my sources are different. And I must talk to you right away."

"Oh, very well, if it's that crucial," Shirley said. "I'll have to let you in myself. I'll watch for your car. When will you get here?"

I consulted my watch. "In fifteen minutes," I said. "I'll be waiting," she said and hung up.

I went upstairs and changed out of my comfortable terry robe and pulled on a pair of jeans and a sweat shirt. I filled Bruno in on where I was going and what I had in mind. He gave me his usual "Yes, Ms. Fein," and I left. Just as I was firing up the Gumdrop, the extension phone in the garage rang. After two rings, it stopped. Obviously, Bruno had picked it up from inside the house. I pulled out of the garage and headed down the drive. In a few minutes, I was entering the grounds of Aphrodite's. I could hardly wait to see the expression on Shirley's face when I told her what I'd learned about lovable Dr. Lucius Keene!

11/ Doris Fein and Her Electric Swimming Pool

Shirley was waiting as I pulled up in front of Aphrodite's. I guess she heard the Gumdrop's engine as I approached. We exchanged pleasantries as we walked down the long corridor to her office. We didn't sit in the living-room section of her office. Shirley went to her desk, and I sat in a chair opposite her.

"Now, then, Doris," she said with a dazzling smile, "tell me what's so important that you couldn't wait until tomorrow evening."

Suddenly, I felt diffident about telling Shirley all that I had unearthed about Dr. Keene. All the arguments that Jerry Kobrin and Larry Small had proposed, explaining in innocent terms what had happened years ago, came flooding back into my mind.

I looked at Shirley, so sweet and obviously concerned about me. How could I say all that I knew without hurting her feelings? Then I thought of Dr. Lucius and his methods. That put some backbone into me. I couldn't have a wonderful person like Shirley victimized by Keene. She might go on for years, never knowing the terrible things he did. Past and present.

"I've found out some things about Dr. Keene that you should know, Shirley," I began.

She raised one perfect eyebrow; then a look of concern crossed her face. "Oh, I do hope that you didn't listen to all of Katy's gossip," she said. "Katy loves gossip so much that when she doesn't have anything juicy to say, she invents things."

"This isn't poolside chatter, Shirley," I said earnestly. "And what's more, I think something has happened to Katy Byrd."

"She seemed fine when she left Aphrodite's," Shirley said. "Considering that she doesn't cooperate with us, she still lost some weight."

Darnit! This was going all wrong. I had a lot of hard evidence of what Dr. Lucius was up to. But Shirley was so sweet and trusting, it occurred to me that she'd never believe it. I put on my best businesslike tone of voice and said, "Shirley, what I'm about to say may seem incredible. I didn't want to believe it myself. But I have reason to believe that Dr. Lucius is a Dr. Feelgood."

"A what, Doris?" she said, puzzled. "I've never heard that expression. What does it mean?"

"It means that he prescribes all sorts of drugs, dangerous ones. They give your guests a false feeling of well-being. But the drugs he's dispensing are addictive. I know. I went through sheer hell for a few days, emotionally, just because I missed my regular injection of JK-4."

"I've seen the lab analysis of JK-4," Shirley said

quickly. "It is definitely not a narcotic, in whole or in part. JK-4 is used in many reputable clinics in Europe."

"But you don't know for sure that the shots he gives *are* JK-4," I insisted. "I believe they're mostly amphetamines. Otherwise, I wouldn't have had the withdrawal symptoms I did."

"That's a serious accusation without proof, Doris," Shirley said, "and I'm glad that you came to me first. I've worked so hard to make all this." She waved her hand around her in a graceful motion. "I like to think that Aphrodite's is the most modern and medically sound establishment in the world."

"I know how you feel about Aphrodite's," I said. "That's why it's so difficult to tell you all this."

"We can easily check the chemical composition of the injections Lucius has been administering," Shirley said. "And I'm sure we will find no irregularities."

"Wait," I said. "There's more."

"Oh, dear," Shirley said. "What else?" She reached across her desk and accidently knocked over a small bud vase that held a single red rose. The water spilled near her desk intercom. She quickly opened a desk drawer and produced a box of tissues. She mopped up the little spill. It was the first ungraceful motion I'd ever seen her make. All this truth about Dr. Keene must have upset her terribly. I felt like an utter heel. But I pressed on.

"Dr. Keene is not what he seems," I said. "He was involved in a death about six years ago."

"My goodness!" Shirley exclaimed. "I saw his professional résumé, and he was extremely well recommended. But doctors *do* lose patients, Doris. And there was no record of a malpractice suit. That would have shown up when he was checked out." She smoothed her already perfect coiffure. "Before I could hire him, the insurance company had to investigate him. There was nothing in their report even vaguely suspicious."

"It wasn't a result of malpractice," I said. "Some people, myself included, feel it was murder!" Her hand flew to her mouth as I began to explain why I thought Dr. Lucius was dangerous. She didn't say a word as I continued my narrative.

"So, as I see it," I said, summing up, "Lucinda Blair was given a local anesthetic, like lidocaine, in a drink, while the party was going on. The anesthetic paralyzed her gag and breathing reflex. Her body couldn't tell whether it was supposed to breathe or swallow. Lucius or an accomplice tapped her on the head and threw her overboard. She couldn't cry out. The lidocaine would have also paralyzed her vocal cords. She must have drowned in record time. When your body can't stop fluids from going down your windpipe, you can choke to death, or drown almost immediately."

"But why, why?" Shirley said, her face stricken.

"My theory is for money," I said. "Bobbie Blair stood to inherit a fortune from her aunt. Once the deed was done, and it may have been Bobbie herself who spiked auntie's drink, she was wide open to blackmail by whoever supplied her with the lidocaine. Or it may even have been succinylcholine chloride in liquid form."

"But Bobbie comes here regularly," Shirley protested.

"She has no choice," I said. "And for all I know, she's also an addict. Made into one by Dr. Lucius Keene. She certainly doesn't have to come here to pay the blackmail. I checked with a legal data bank, via computer. Bobbie Blair signed a power of attorney five years ago. To none other than Dr. Lucius Keene."

"Oh, no!" Shirley said in horror. "When did you find all this out, Doris?"

"Just tonight, about the power of attorney," I replied. "I learned about the Lucinda Blair affair several days ago." I hesitated. I didn't want Shirley to think that I'd been blabbing her business all over town, so I didn't mention I'd already discussed the matter with Larry, Jerry Kobrin, and Bruno. "I came over as soon as I found out," I said.

"And I'm so glad that you did, Doris, dear," Shirley said. "But now we have a grave problem."

"What's that?" I asked.

"Figuring out what to do with you," said Shirley. She reached down to her desk drawer. I thought she was going for another tissue. But when her hand reappeared, she wasn't holding a tissue. It was a nasty-looking little nickel-plated automatic pistol!

"I'm sure we can think of something," said a familiar voice. I spun around in my chair, and there, standing by the door, was lovable, deadly Dr. Lucius Keene. Mario, the masseur, stood alongside him, with a particularly evil smile on his face.

"Shirley . . ." I began.

"Dear, sweet, Shirley," she mocked. "You just couldn't bring yourself to believe I knew all about

Lucius, eh?" She laughed. "I ought to," she said. "It was my plan to begin with."

"I told you the hypnotherapy would pay off," Dr. Keene said, coming over to where I sat. "She's so brainwashed that she still can't believe you aren't a plaster saint, Shirley."

"The headboard speakers!" I cried.

"Exactly," said Keene with an oily grin. "You should hear the complete tape sometime. It's a masterpiece of its sort. I'm proud of it."

"I'm not proud of the sloppy way you've handled this, Lucius," said Shirley, her nice-Nelly tone disappearing. "Now what are we going to do?"

"Get rid of her, of course," Mario chimed in.

"That goes without saying, you musclebound clod," Shirley snapped. "The question is how?"

"If I may," Lucius said, "I think I have the answer."

"It better be good," Shirley said ominously. "I've had about enough of your bungling, Lucius."

"We have to go down to the pool," he said. "I'll explain along the way. In the meantime, Mario, go out and check the parking lot. I want to make sure that our friend here came alone."

"*Sí*, right away," Mario said and loped off.

"What do you have in mind?" I asked. "Another drowning? You can't get away with that. I won't drink any succinylcholine."

"I wouldn't use it," said Dr. Keene from behind me. "Nor would I inject it. This isn't Spain. Accidental deaths require autopsies in this state. In Spain, doctors are few, and overworked. They did a postmortem there, too. But they weren't looking for lidocaine. Once they found the salt water in Lucinda Blair's lungs, that was it. Even a country doctor could spot that her head injury wasn't a fatal one. Or even enough to render her unconscious."

"How much press can you stand?" I asked. "I'm a prominent citizen of this town. I own a newspaper. You'll have Jerry Kobrin, the crime reporter, up here as soon as the news is out. And I lied to you, Shirley. I told him all about my suspicions."

"Oh, I doubt that," Shirley said, prodding me toward the pool area. "Otherwise, you wouldn't have come alone. That is, if you did come here alone."

The intercom phone rang, and Keene walked over to the wall where the phone was. He spoke a few seconds and returned to Shirley and me at poolside with a self-satisfied smile on his face.

"That was Mario," he said. "She's alone. No other cars in sight."

"As to the prying press," Lucius continued, "I'm not worried. You see, when your body is discovered, I'll be miles away. On my Christmas vacation. I left here yesterday, didn't I, Shirley?"

"Yes, that's right, Lucius," Shirley agreed. "Now, what's your plan?"

"Simplicity, itself. Once Mario gets back, he will begin servicing our pool. The shutdown over the holidays allows us to do maintenance on our equipment."

"Get to the point, Lucius," Shirley said.

"Really, my dear," Keene said, "I should think we owe Doris the courtesy of knowing exactly how she's

going to die. And how all of us will get away with it."
The doors to the pool area opened and Mario came in.

"You're going to be implicated, too," I said to Mario.
"Your picture was in the paper, along with Dr. Keene's
—*Señor* Arruza. You're no Frenchman, despite your
phony accent."

"I think of myself as a citizen of the world," Mario
said airily. Then to Lucius, he said, "I looked over her
car. I'm familiar with the Triumph sports model. I can
rig the brakes. She can have a fatal accident."

"How, you dunce?" Lucius Keene said shortly. "Off
a mountain road? This whole area is flat as a pancake!
Shut up and listen to me.

"First, go to the fuse box for the main house. I want
you to disconnect the circuit for the pool lights." Mario
turned to go. "Wait, you idiot!" called Keene. "I'm not
done yet. While you're at the fuse box, pick up a heavy
screwdriver or a pry bar. And put on your bathing suit.
Now, go!"

Mario took off, and Lucius Keene came over to me.
He put a hand on my shoulder. I shrank away in horror.

"Don't be upset, my dear," he said. "It will all be over
soon. When Mario comes back, he will get into the deep
end of the pool. Using a pry bar, he will loosen the cover
on the underwater pool light near the diving board.
Those pool lights run on two hundred and twenty volts.
Then, once he is out of the water, he will reconnect the
circuit. The end of the pool nearest the light will be
heavily charged with electricity."

Just then, the lights in the pool went out. "Excellent,"
Keene chortled. "Mario has found the proper fuse.

Now, where was I? Oh, yes. Then we strip you, Doris, and drop you into the pool. The electricity will render you unconscious and you will drown. No drugs to be traced, no bruises or other signs of violence.

"It's already known that you have permission to use the facilities at any time. The receptionist and staff have a memo from Shirley to that effect. They've had it for weeks. No premeditation there, you see. Just an unfortunate coincidence. Now, I'm afraid I must leave you. I want to be miles from here, in a place where I'll be seen when all this happens."

"Leaving Mario and me to do the dirty work?" Shirley asked pointedly.

"Use your pretty head, my dear," Dr. Lucius said. "I've been involved in one society drowning before. We don't want the slightest hint of suspicion. And how can you be implicated? Mario was working on the pool. You didn't know that. You gave Doris permission to use the pool and you stayed in your office. By the time you began to wonder about our own dear Doris, and went to the pool, it was too late."

"But there'll be a lawsuit. A huge one!" Shirley protested.

"It doesn't matter," Keene said. "We'd have to shut down the spa anyhow. If it's found out that Bobbie Blair is dead . . ."

"What?" I squeaked.

"Oh, yes, you didn't know about that," Shirley said. "Once she had signed the power of attorney, we thought we'd have no trouble with her. She was thoroughly addicted, though. That meant that sooner or later she'd have run afoul of the authorities in her world travels. We couldn't take that chance. Lucius gave her an overdose, and we disposed of her remains. Alongside of her is your talky friend, Mrs. Byrd."

"You didn't!" I cried.

"Oh, but we *did*," said Keene. "She'll disappear on the same route our Bobbie Blair impersonator took. First Rio, then who knows where? Her signature is no problem for Mario. He's a man of many talents. It runs in his family. In fact, the woman impersonating Bobbie Blair is Mario's sister. She'll hire someone to be Katy Byrd and will travel with her. By then, she'll have mastered Byrd's childish scrawl."

"What did you do with the bodies?" I asked.

"I told you I had a complete laboratory here," Lucius Keene said. "I devised an acid bath. I disposed of what the acid didn't destroy in a novel way. We recently had the tennis court repaved. Katy and Bobbie are under it. And a good thing, too. I had to store what was left of Blair in a plastic bag until our holiday shutdown. I hadn't intended it to be a double ceremony of interment. It just worked out that way, happily."

"You monster!" I hissed. "Don't you have *any* human feelings?"

"Certainly," said Keene. "I enjoy the life of a wealthy man. I like fine wines and cognac, good food, and tailored suits. I appreciate fine art. And frankly, once you've done one murder, the rest come easy. I have nothing to lose. I lost my ethics six years ago, on a yacht off Spain. Thanks to your dear, innocent Shirley."

"Don't tell me I corrupted you, Lucius," Shirley retorted. "You were in debt up to your ears from the casino at Monte Carlo. You were already selling drugs to an elite circle of society."

"But I'd never killed anyone," protested Lucius Keene. "Not until you got your claws into me."

"The slow death of addiction doesn't count, I suppose," I put in.

"A fine distinction, Doris," he said. "One doesn't have to kill an addict. They kill themselves. They would have obtained the stuff elsewhere. I merely saved them the embarrassment and inconvenience."

"You're making yourself sound like a positive humanitarian," I said.

"In a way, I am," Lucius Keene said, nodding. "The horrors of withdrawal need never be faced. I have an unlimited supply, all legal. And then, there are all the women whose lives I have made happier, through this place. . . ." He turned to Mario, who had come up next to him, and quickly explained what to do. The masseur, clad in a tiny male bikini, slipped into the pool. He reached over the side and grabbed his screwdriver, and disappeared under the surface of the water.

"What about him?" Shirley asked, indicating the bubbles rising from the bottom of the pool.

"He's about reached the limit of his usefulness," Keene said, "What I'd suggest . . ." He broke off as Mario surfaced.

"I have the cover off the light," he said, wiping the water from his eyes.

"Good, good," Keene said. "Now, carefully—I don't want this messed up—pinch the *green* wire on the light between the cover and the insulation for the light. Make sure that the insulation on the wire is broken. Just screwing down the lid should do that. But check and make sure."

"This would go easier and faster if I had a face mask," Mario said.

"And even faster if you had gills," Lucius said, "but you don't. Get moving. We haven't all night." Mario again dived below the waters.

"As I was saying," said Lucius, peering into the water where Mario was working, "once we get rid of Doris, tell Mario to pull her body out of the water. But before you do, turn the power back on. . . ."

Mario came up again. "All set," he said.

"Excellent, Mario," Keene said. "Now go to the basement and turn the power back on. We'll get Ms. Fein ready for her final swim." Mario went off through the double doors at the far end of the pool room.

"You'll be rid of him that way," Keene continued. "He came into the pool area and saw Doris. He dived in to save her, and he, too, got a jolt and drowned."

"Makes sense," Shirley agreed. "And we don't have to split the Blair fortune with him, either. His sister shouldn't be a problem. If the money to live like Bobbie Blair keeps coming in, she'll stay quiet."

"Now I must be going," Lucius Keene said. "I want to be far away. Give me about twenty minutes to a half hour." He turned to me. "So sorry, Doris, that I won't be here when you take your last swim. I won't even get to see how slim your body will look in the water. I'm rather proud of you. You lost all the weight you wanted to. And now, farewell." He gave me a cheery wave and began strolling toward the pool doors.

"All right, Doris," Shirley said, waving the pistol. "Strip!"

"Why should I?" I said. "What will you do if I don't? Shoot me? I'm a dead woman right now. I won't make it easier for you!"

Shirley sighed. "I can simply have Mario strip you down," she said. "I don't have to shoot you. But if I must, I will. It will only complicate things, that's all."

I looked around the pool area. There was no place to run. In fact, there was nothing I could use for a weapon. As slowly as I could, I pulled off my sweat shirt with the picture of Felix Mendelssohn on it.

"That's a sensible girl," Shirley said in a soothing tone. "I'm truly sorry it ended this way, Doris." She went to the wall and got down the long aluminum pole and net that's used to fish out objects that fall into the pool. "Stand by the edge, dear," she commanded. I was hoping that she'd set down the little pistol when she reached for the pole and net, but she didn't. She tucked it under one arm and advanced toward me. "Take off the rest of your clothing, Doris," she ordered. "It will be over in a second."

"It sure will, lady," said a voice. "And if you move a hair, I'll have to shoot you."

My gaze was on Shirley. I had been like a bird being stalked by a snake. I turned and saw the most welcome sight I've ever seen. At the doors to the pool stood Sheriff Jaime Ortega, with his service revolver aimed straight at Shirley. On either side of the sheriff were Larry Small and Jerry Kobrin!

"I'll go quietly," Shirley said. She raised her arm slightly, and the pistol pressed to her body fell to the floor with a clatter. Jaime Ortega holstered his gun and walked toward her.

Shirley turned to me, her eyes blazing with hatred. "You rotten little snoop!" she snarled. "You've spoiled it all."

Suddenly, with an animal cry, she rushed at me, the pool cleaning pole lowered like a lance. It caught me in the pit of my stomach. I saw Jaime grab for his pistol again as I teetered on the edge of the electrified swimming pool. I clawed air, desperately trying to regain my balance. Just as Larry Small rushed to my side, I lost my equilibrium completely, and fell backward into the deadly waters below!

12/ On the Road to Nesselrode

Nothing happened. Oh, I don't mean that I didn't sink into the pool, or that I bounced off the surface of the water. I went in all right. But there was no jolt of electricity. Not that I would have known what to expect. Getting a terminal electric shock is a sensation that can't be described. At least no one has ever survived to tell what it felt like.

I came up to the surface and swam to the side of the pool. Things got busy for a few seconds. Jaime Ortega threw a restraining judo hold on Shirley. Larry rushed to the poolside and offered me a hand. It was then that I realized I was naked from the waist up.

"My sweat shirt," I said. "Give it to me."

"You gonna put it on underwater?" Larry said with a grin.

"Turn your back, then," I said.

"What for?" Larry asked. "I've been standing at the pool doors for quite some time now, Dee."

140

I shrugged mentally and, disdaining the hand Larry offered, got out of the pool. Sopping wet, I sloshed over to where my sweat shirt lay and pulled it on. Feeling a bit more covered, I turned to regard the tableau unfolding.

One of Jaime Ortega's deputies appeared from the far end of the pool area with Mario in tow. Still another came through the doors at the opposite end with Dr. Lucius in handcuffs. Jaime was putting a set of manacles on Shirley. Jerry Kobrin was asking questions of anyone who'd answer.

Seeing an opportunity to exit gracefully, I went into the anteroom to the sauna and found what I was looking for. An Aphrodite exercise suit. It wasn't my size. I had to roll up the cuffs on the pants and jacket, but at least I wasn't sopping wet. Barefoot, I went back to the pool. As I came back to where the suspects were being herded off, Shirley was railing at both Mario and Lucius Keene. The language was worthy of a longshoreman. But loosely translated from the obscene and the profane, it went like this:

"Mario, you stupid clod! A simple job and you screwed it up! Can't you tell one color wire from another?"

"I did what Lucius said," Mario replied sullenly. "He made the mistake."

"You wouldn't know your elbow from third base, you cut-rate Romeo," Keene replied. Except he didn't say *elbow.*

Jaime Ortega had been inspecting the deep end of the pool by leaning over its edge. He got to his feet. "Blame each other all you want," he said with a smile.

"It wasn't Mario's fault. He worked with the pool lights out. His only light source was the fixtures in this room. The bottom and sides of the pool are painted blue. In that kind of light, the yellow wire, the ground wire, looks green. The blue wire looks off-cream color. All he did was ground the pool light. And that blew the fuse almost as soon as he threw the switch for the power."

Jaime noticed me coming through the sauna doors.

"Are you all right, Doris?" he asked.

"Fine, but damp," I said. "Which is better than being damp and dead." I turned to Larry. "How did you get here?" I asked.

"Funny you should ask," Larry said jokingly. He came over and put his arms around me. "You owe it to my curiosity and to John Perry, the photographer.

"I went back to the *Register* office after I left you downtown," he said. "I wanted to see more of the morgue and chat a bit with Jerry. That's when John came in with the positive print he had made from the wirephoto. The picture that ran with the story of Lucinda Blair's death. He had some other pictures from the file, too. Stuff that wasn't used. One of the shots had the full guest list. The other people who were aboard. There was a picture of Shirley among them. I was excited about what he'd found, so I telephoned your house."

"And Bruno told you where I was?" I asked in wonder.

"Not at first," Larry admitted. "He just told me that you weren't at home. Then I asked him if he knew where you'd gone. He said yes. Then I had to ask him to tell me. That's when I found out where you'd gone."

"It was lucky you asked him the way you did," I said. "You'd have never found out otherwise."

"I know. He doesn't volunteer much information," Larry said. "However, I *am* a trained interviewer. When I found out you'd gone to warn Shirley about Lucius Keene, not knowing she was part of the whole sordid mess, I got Jaime Ortega on the phone right away. Jerry drove me out here."

"You got here in plenty of time, then," I said. "Why did you wait so long before stopping Shirley? I could have been killed. It was just Mario's goof that saved me."

"We couldn't make a move, Doris," Jaime Ortega put in. "Not as long as Shirley was holding that gun on you. If we'd busted in, she could have held us off, using you as a hostage. I couldn't risk it."

"So you risked me taking an electric swim?" I retorted. "Some choice."

"It was a gamble," admitted the sheriff. "But I figured we could fish you out of the pool and give you mouth-to-mouth resuscitation. A bullet is more dangerous."

"I volunteered for the mouth-to-mouth part," Larry said. "And I think I got cheated out of my chance."

"That's easily remedied," I said. I threw my arms around him and planted one of my sultrier kisses on his lips.

"I'll have seconds on the wild rice and duck, Bruno," said my Uncle Saul. Bruno obligingly restocked my uncle's plate.

"That's thirds," said Aunt Ceil, "but who's counting?"

"Unkind, unkind," said Uncle Saul, grinning.

"And you're not exactly wasting away, Ceil," I chimed in.

"Is that what's called a skinnier-than-thou attitude?" asked Jerry Kobrin. "If so, it doesn't make me feel the least bit guilty. On a reporter's pay, you don't get a crack at orange-stuffed roast duck with Grand Marnier sauce. Not often, anyway." He addressed himself to his own third helping.

"I don't understand you people," my mother said. "Here you are, feeding your faces, when only three days ago Doris was almost killed by that horrible woman and her accomplices."

"More like partners, Mother," I corrected. "They all had a share in the Blair fortune and Aphrodite's."

"I don't care about their finances," my mother came back. "I care about my daughter. And I can't see how you were so taken in by that scheming woman. Doris, you're usually so perceptive about people."

"Not her fault, Mrs. Fein," Larry said, from my right side. "Doris couldn't help it. Each night for two weeks, she was being brainwashed while she slept."

"I had no idea that hypnotraining could be so effective," my father said. "I've read papers on it in medical journals, and it shouldn't have worked so efficiently."

"It wouldn't have," Larry conceded, "except that in order for Doris to be able to sleep after all the speed they shot into her, she was given a strong hypnotic drug with her evening meals. With the drug breaking down her normal resistance, and her being exhausted by the exercise, the hypnoconditioning worked like a charm.

Doris thought of Shirley as a cross between a saint and the Easter Bunny."

"Ecumenically stated simile," Jerry said with a smile. "However, I get your drift."

My mother wouldn't be denied her thesis. "Still and all, Doris," she went on, "you should have had some feeling; some intuition about her."

"In a way, it may have been your fault, Mother," I said.

"Well, I like that! I barely see you these days, since you inherited this fortune. How could I be to blame?"

"By being yourself," I replied. "Do you remember when all you could do or say was Serena, Serena, Serena? You did your hair like her. You wore the styles she did."

"What of it? Millions of other women were doing the same thing."

"But they didn't live in the same house with me," I said in triumph. "The reason I was a sitting duck for her brainwashing was simple. She reminded me of you, my role model when I was young. She was a mother figure to me."

"Now, at *that* I draw the line!" Linda Fein said huffily. "Comparing me to a murderess!"

"No, Mother," I said gently. "Comparing you to the most chic and beautiful woman in the world."

"For her day, of course," put in Aunt Ceil cattily.

"All's well, and you know the rest," said my father.

"I just hope that you've learned from the experience," Uncle Saul said. "If you're constitutionally a heavy person, don't fool with Mother Nature."

"I knew I wanted to tell you something, Dee-Dee," my father said with a big grin. "I spoke with Dr. Mc-Donald at the Medical Center today. About what the drugs might have done to your system."

"What did he say?"

"No damage whatever," Dad replied. "Except for one side effect."

"Oh, no!" I said. "Did the drugs harm me in some way?"

"Indirectly," Dad said. "From all the exercise and dieting, a strange thing has happened."

"For the love of heaven, Michael," my mother said, "don't keep us all hanging. What did Dr. Ron say?"

"That Doris should have checked with him about her ideal weight for her frame. She was, indeed, over-weight when she went to see him for the checkup. But Doris"—he waggled a finger at me—"you never both-ered to find out exactly what you should weigh. When you went back to Ron McDonald, he was appalled at your figure. You went too far with your weight loss."

I heard a grumble of triumph from Petunia. I didn't need the reminder. I had a good idea of what Dad was going to say. "You mean to tell me . . . ?" I asked.

"That's right, honey," Dad said. "For your frame and general bone structure, you are at present about ten pounds *under*weight!" He got to his feet. "And if I am to remain at my own sensible weight, I can't stay seated here at the moaning board. Anyone for a game of pocket billiards? Eight Ball, last pocket's my game."

"I'll be the pigeon," Uncle Saul said, getting up. "I'm beginning to feel guilty with all this diet talk."

The company got up and drifted toward the billiard room. Maybe the diet talk was catching. Nobody bothered with dessert. Larry and I stayed seated. We looked at each other in silence for a while.

"I guess that answers the question about whether the mother-to-mother network is still trying to marry us off to each other," Larry said. "Everyone got up on cue to leave us alone."

"There are other people whose company wouldn't be as pleasing to me," I said.

"If that was a compliment, thanks," Larry said.

"I owe you my life, Larry," I said. "If you hadn't arrived when you did, I would have been another unfortunate 'accident' at Aphrodite's."

"Yeah, but you did all the research and brainwork, Dee," he said. "I just made a few phone calls and rounded up the cavalry." He reached over and took my hand. "But I must admit, we make a good team."

I didn't miss the implication. All the insecurities came crowding back. Was Larry Small interested in me personally? Or was Harry's money going to be a stumbling block between us, as it had been between Carl Suzuki and me?

As though he'd read my mind, Larry asked, "So have you made up your mind about the money? I mean, what do you intend to do with all the loot Harry left you?"

"Glad you asked," I said. "Some of it, I'm going to give to charities. Whatever is on the top of my mother's list. Then there's this house. I've realized why I'm not comfortable around here."

"You're not going to sell it?" Larry gulped.

"I can't," I replied. "Part of Harry's will specifies that I have to live in it. Not that it's a hardship. But what made it uncomfortable was not understanding Bruno. I do now. Second, the place is like Harry Grubb's tomb. There hasn't been a young person living here since Harry restored it. I'm going to change all that. I went over to Dale Vista sanitarium to see Helen Grayson. In a month or so, she'll be able to face the world again."

"She used to teach piano to underprivileged kids at no charge. I remember her concerts at the high school auditorium. Some of those kids were great," Larry recalled.

"Exactly," I said. "But she had just so much time to give to them. She had to teach untalented kids like me to support her budding geniuses. I'm going to change that. I spoke to her doctor, and he thinks it would be great therapy for Helen. I'm going to open a free music school for any kid who shows talent. Lord knows, I have the room here."

"That's wonderful, Dee," Larry said. "But can Mrs. Grayson handle such a work load?"

"She won't be alone," I said. "I'll hire other teachers. And this old mausoleum will be filled with kids and music. I'll have a live-in staff, too. Harry's art works are lovely, but they shouldn't be locked away here. I'm donating a bunch of them to the Bowers Museum, in Santa Ana. The Grubb Collection, it'll be called."

"Why not the Doris Fein Collection?"

"Because they belonged to Harry. I didn't acquire a one of them. I have time to get my own stuff. But all this money talk is a bore. What about you? Are you going back to San Francisco after New Year's?"

"You *are* intuitive," Larry said. "No, I'm not, Dee. I'm fed up with the whole pop music scene."

"Can this be the same Larry Small who used to eat, sleep, and breathe rock?" I asked in mock wonder.

"The very same person," Larry said. "No, I take that back."

"What brought about the change?"

"Well, Dee," Larry said, "it's like the kid that gets turned loose in a candy store after a life of poverty. They tell him: 'Go get it, kid.' And in a few days, the kid can't look at candy anymore and has a king-size belly-ache. That's what I've got. An artistic bellyache. I know I'm a good writer and a good reporter. But somehow, covering record-store openings and interviewing punk rockers isn't my idea of what a mature person should be doing for a living."

"What do you want to do, then?" I asked.

"I dunno, Dee. I'm not hurting financially. My *Dr. Doom* book is selling just great. I got an offer for film rights on it. Some company wants to make it into a movie."

"That's wonderful!" I cried.

"That's money, that's all it is." Larry smiled ruefully. "I wouldn't be writing the screenplay. I wouldn't know how to start. No, I don't want to trade the rat race I'm in for the Hollywood rat race. I don't know how to say it, but I want to do something worthwhile. The only hangup is, I don't know what." He fiddled with his coffee cup. "I'd be ready to work on *The Register*, tomorrow," Larry said. "But I know that's not possible."

"Who says so?" I came back quickly. "I own *The Register*. I can see to it you're hired!"

"That's not how I want to get a job," Larry said. "I can see it now: Childhood sweetheart of publisher gets cushy job on her newspaper."

"It wouldn't be like that, and you know it, Larry Small. You'd earn every cent."

"You know that, and I know that," Larry said. "But would the rest of the world? And more important, would the rest of the staff on *The Register*?"

"They'd know as soon as they saw the quality of your writing," I said. "And you do have credentials. A year on *Rolling Stone,* a best-selling novel . . ."

"I'd have to think about it, Dee," Larry said. "It would have to be a real job, not a silly feature."

"How about investigative reporting?" I asked. "This Aphrodite affair has opened my eyes. There are scores of ripoff artists at work, and not only in the health and beauty field. There are gangs of crooks who take the public for millions each year. You could unmask them, Larry."

"Mmmmm," Larry said reflectively. "Sort of like a Ralph Nader with a column. . . ."

"I was thinking more along the lines of a David Horowitz," I said, "but you get the idea."

"I sure do, Dee. I think it's a great idea. But one thing . . ."

"Yes?"

"The first time there's any chatter about me not being competent to do my work, I walk out."

"The first time you're not competent to do your work, you won't have to. Dave Rose will fire you. Nobody sits on my payroll without delivering."

"Then you, my skinny lady," Larry said, extending his hand, "have just hired yourself a reporter." He got up and I stood as well. "Shall we see how badly your dad is beating your Uncle Saul at Eight Ball?" Laughing, we went into the billiard room.

Hours later, I sat in my room, after entering the day's news into Harry's unsolved-crime file, with Bruno's aid. It gave me great satisfaction to remove the Blair case from the unsolved file. I had also entered the day's events into my diary. I looked at my bedside alarm clock. Its digital face read half past one in the morning. Late. Very late. In all probability, Bruno had retired for the night. I felt a deep-seated rumble begin in the pit of my stomach. The voice of Petunia. Then I had a sudden inspiration.

I picked up the intercom phone and rang the kitchen. No answer. I wrapped my terry cloth robe around me and went out of my room and down the hall to the second-floor landing. There were only a few night lights on below. Wrapping my robe so that I wouldn't get any banister burns, I swung a leg over the railing and whooped my way down to the main floor. Then I made for the kitchen. I happened to know that Bruno had made a Nesselrode pie and a chocolate soufflé for the dessert no one had touched. After all, I *was* ten pounds underweight. And a young woman should keep her strength up. . . .